Published by:
Powder River Publishing LLC
1014 Black Mountain Road
Thermopolis, Wyoming 82443

Copyright © 2025
ISBN: 978-1-956881-55-4
Printed in the United States of America

Dedication

Contents

Introduction

There are different theories about Bigfoot (Sasquatch).

It is known to be a shy creature; as some say.

Others believe it can be aggressive.

This is about a farm couple and their experience with Bigfoot.

They are cattle farmers raising beef cows.

Joe and Alex are in their fifties and live alone since their kids are grown and have families of their own.

The couple learns about the existence of Bigfoot on their property. They learn more about the creature as they try to figure out how to share the property.

Accidentally killing a Bigfoot leads them on a path that most wouldn't believe and nobody wants to follow.

Joe and Alex take turns hunting during the deer season in Pennsylvania so someone is there to take care of the farm chores each day.

They have a dairy cow that they milk for their own use.

They make cheese, butter, and occasionally yogurt when they have more milk than the two of them can consume.

Chapter 1
The Hunt

It's four o'clock in the morning on the opening day of the Antlered Deer season, Buck season as it is more commonly referred to in Pennsylvania.

Joe (short for Joseph) is getting ready for his hunt.

Joe's wife Alex (short for Alexandria) is helping him get ready.

Joe has had game cameras set up watching a certain buck all summer and the weeks leading up to opening day.

He knows the time frame the buck goes through the area where he had the cameras placed and is certain he will get this large ten point buck.

Joe and Alex have a farm and grow hay and corn.

Joe kisses Alex as he leaves with his hunting gear.

He has his rifle and a lunch that Alex packed for him. A thermos of coffee and a few bottles of water as well. He has his license, a pen to fill out the tag, a full box of ammunition; just in case he misses he has more ammunition. He has a rope to drag the deer out to the field so he can return with his pickup to take it to the house. He has his hunting knife and he has a flashlight so he can see to get to his stand before day break.

Joe walks slowly trying to be quiet as he walks to his stand.

He doesn't want to scare the deer that he can't see in the dark.

He is listening, as well, to the noises in the predawn hour. He knows there is a black bear in the area but doesn't know its travel pattern.

All the pictures of the bear he has seen on the trail cameras, he has never seen any cubs. But he is not ruling out the possibility of it having cubs. So he is really trying not to surprise the bear at all. He keeps his light swinging side to side as he walks.

At the edge of the hay field he sees eye shine at the tree line.

It is too far away to see what it is. The eye shine doesn't seem right to him to be a deer. So he hesitates with the light on the eyes. He continues slowly, one step at a time, hoping to see what it is and praying it is not the bear. He is praying it is not a mountain lion or a bobcat either. Although, he would prefer one of the cats over the bear.

Joe stops and loads his rifle, just in case he needs it to defend himself.

He is thinking it might be the bear, but still isn't close enough to see it in the light.

He continues slowly.

The eyes disappear.

Joe stops and shines the light around the area to see if he can find the eyes again or better still the animal itself.

After a few minutes he continues walking toward his stand.

Joe gets to his stand and stands there shining his light around and doesn't see any eye shine and no animal shapes in the light, so he climbs up into the tree stand.

As he is climbing he notices some of the rungs on the ladder are damaged. Not broken but damaged. He figures the bear damaged the ladder, it wouldn't be the first time a bear destroyed his tree stand.

Joe gets settled into his stand and sits there waiting for day light, listening to the sounds.

The sun rises and he can start to see the area.

He notices something about one hundred yards from his stand.

Kind of sticking out from under the brush. Almost like it was being hidden.

As the sun continues to rise he can see it is the back end of a deer.

He looks around for the bear, or the mountain lion.

He doesn't see either of them and so he waits and watches.

Joe hears movement in the heavy brush where he can't see.

He raises his rifle ready if the buck comes out.

He sees the bear come out of the brush so he lowers his rifle but keeps it in hand just in case the bear decides he is on the menu this morning.

The bear walks over to the deer and sniffs it.

The bear sniffs around the bush and then runs away.

Joe is confused, he can't think of any reason a bear would leave an easy meal let alone run from it.

One reason he can think of is if the kill belongs to a larger bear.

He thought this bear was big, estimating the weight about four hundred pounds maybe four hundred fifty.

Joe isn't aware of another bear in the area. But knows one could have wondered into the area or perhaps the game commission officers released a larger bear on the neighbor's property recently and it came into his hunting area.

So again he sits and waits. He sees squirrels, small birds and chipmunks all around his stand but no deer.

He drinks a little coffee every so often. Trying not to drink too much at one time in an attempt to delay the urge to urinate as long as possible.

Back at the house Alex is getting the items out to butcher the deer when Joe returns with one. She gets the meat grinder out, the seasoning to make bologna, the meat saw. The knives they use to butcher.

She starts the chores after she has everything out of its off season storage area.

This is the time of the year when they take turns hunting. So the daily choirs still get done each day. She has a different area of the farm that she hunts deer on the other side of the property from where Joe hunts.

She feeds the dogs, cats and then goes to the barn to milk the one dairy cow they have for their own milk. They have beef cattle in the pasture.

They use the milk to make their own butter, cheese, occasionally yogurt though not often because she is the only one that eats yogurt since the kids moved out. They will make yogurt if they know the kids are going to visit with the grandkids. They also make their own ice cream, but again not all the time. It depends on the amount of milk they need to use up before it spoils.

When she is done milking the cow she returns to the house and, using the old method with a cheese cloth, she strains the milk before putting it in the refrigerator.

Once the milk is in the refrigerator she decides she is going to bake an apple pie with some of the apples they gathered from the apple tree.

Joe can cook but he is not a baker so Alex does the baking.

She turns on the radio: that they keep tuned to their preferred local country station: and gets started peeling, coring and slicing the apples. Then she mixes the apple slices and sugar together for the filling, and then begins making the dough for the pie crust from scratch. She makes two pies.

She places the pies in the oven to bake and refrigerates the left over apples.

Joe is in his stand and hasn't seen anything since the bear. He is not surprised by that at all and is still hopeful of seeing the deer he is after still today.

It's now noon and so he opens his lunch bag and takes out a sandwich and begins eating it.

He hears movement, which he figured would happen as soon as he opened his sandwich, so he places his sandwich on the bag next to him and is watching for the animal to show itself.

He sees the mountain lion come out and walk over to the deer in the brush.

So now he is thinking that the mountain lion killed the deer. So he watches and retrieves his sandwich and eats while watching the mountain lion. He does think it is odd that if this is the mountain lions kill, it isn't buried the way they normally would. Unless he spooked the cat on his way in to his stand this morning.

The mountain lion appears to hesitate at the deer.

The cat is looking around and up in the trees. Looks right at Joe and stares. Joe remains motionless and the cat continues looking around.

The cat is showing signs of being nervous and perhaps scared. Joe can see the nervousness of the cat's behavior but isn't sure about it being scared. He is reading the body language like he does his farm cats when they get nervous.

Joe continues to watch the cat, figuring he isn't going to see a deer while the mountain lion is nearby.

Joe does look around from time to time just to see if there is anything moving through the woods.

The mountain lion grabs the hind quarter of the deer and begins to drag it out of the brush.

After the cat has the deer out of the brush and Joe can see it is a young spike buck. He hears a loud, deep, horrifying roar, is the only way he can think to describe the sound. He doesn't know how else to explain the sound to himself let alone try to explain it to someone else. The sound shakes him to his core; he can feel it as well as hear the deafening sound.

The cat runs, leaving a distinct path in the leaves as it goes. He could easily track the cat if he wanted too.

Joe is curious, he has never heard that sound before and knows of no animal that makes that sound.

He is looking around trying to see what made that sound and trying not to move any more than he needs to.

He gets wind of a scent that he is not familiar with. It is a very strong odor, musty, moldy; what he believes to be a hint of decay as well, he is having trouble trying to identify the odor. What he knows for sure is that it is a foul and unpleasant odor.

He turns his attention in the direction the wind is coming from. Knowing the odor is being carried by the wind.

He can hear something coming. It sounds big.

He keeps watching.

A very large creature is approaching; and is trying to hide behind trees as it approaches.

Joe knows there should be nobody on his property. He and Alex have not given permission to anyone to hunt the property. But who would hunt with such an offensive odor?

Joe begins to think about the stories he has heard; the shows he has watched about Bigfoot. About the odor, the loud roar and the size of the creature.

He raises his rifle slowly, not wanting to scare the creature.

He looks at the creature with the help of the scope on his rifle.

He sees why he has heard about people who have not been able to pull the trigger after looking at the face. It appears to have human features; covered with hair and hard to determine for sure.

The creature stops and walks away from him, back in the direction it came from.

Joe is completely confused. He has never believed in Bigfoot, but there it was, he has no other explanation for what he has seen.

He remains in his stand the rest of the day and never sees the buck he is after.

With the last bit of sunlight he climbs out of his stand and heads back to the house.

He looks over his shoulder every so often just to be sure the creature isn't following him. He remembers some stories where the

Bigfoot follows the people. But he never sees anything behind him. As he enters the house and takes his boots off. Alex sets the food on the table.

She asks what he has seen, if he ever saw the big buck.

They sit at the table and he tells her no big buck. But a dead spike about one hundred yards from his stand, give or take a few yards.

He continues to tell her about the bear and the mountain lion with the dead deer.

When he tells her about the roar she just stares at him.

He isn't sure what to think about her silence. He isn't able to read her face to see if she even believes him.

She speaks up before he says anything else, "Did you see what made that sound?"

Joe nods his head, "Yes."

Alex, "What was it?"

Joe, "Bigfoot, is the only way I know how to describe it."

Alex, "I have heard that sound before but thought I was hearing an animal that I couldn't identify."

Joe looks at her, "When did you hear it?"

Alex, "A couple weeks ago while milking the cow in the evening. You hadn't returned from your ammo run."

Joe, "Why didn't you tell me?"

Alex lets out a little laugh, "You wouldn't have believed me and would have figured the same thing I did, that it was an animal that I didn't know."

Joe nods and shrugs his shoulders at the same time, "You are most likely right. I still don't know if I believe what I saw. The face was very human like, just covered with hair."

Alex tilts her head a little to one side, "I thought they looked more ape like in the face."

Joe, "So did I but, remember, some of the shows we watched that had pictures of the face? Some of them were human like in the face."

Alex nods her head to agree.

As they finish supper and begin to clear the table.

Alex, "Why didn't you shoot it?"

Joe shakes his head, "It looked to human. I understand those shows we saw that the individual said they couldn't shoot it because it looked human."

Alex, "So you want me to shoot it if I see it?"

Joe, "That is up to you babe. But when you look at it in your scope you will see what I mean."

Alex, "Yeah, but the money we could get could be a big help to us."

Joe, "I know."

Alex, "Do you think it would be in my area tomorrow?"

Joe, "Hard to say, nobody knows the territory range of the creature or their behavior at all."

Alex nods again while she thinks.

Alex, "I think I'm going to take the 357 mag pistol with me tomorrow as well. That way I have it for protection if I can't use the rifle for some reason."

Joe, "Ok."

They get the dishes done and watch tv for a couple hours and then go to bed.

The alarm goes off at four o'clock again and they get Alex packed and on her way to her stand next to the corn field.

She has a road to walk next to the field between the corn and the woods.

She has her flashlight going side to side as well scanning for anything that might be within range of the light.

She gets to her stand without seeing anything.

She climbs the ladder into her tree stand and listens to the sounds in the dark.

As the sun comes up she can see deer coming her way on the road between the corn and the tree line.

She uses her scope to verify if they have antlers or not and they do not, so her hunt will last longer today.

A couple of hours later the same deer, she suspects, are running as fast as they can back to the corn field.

She hears the deer running through the corn hitting the stalks as they go through the field. She can even see the stalks move as the deer run.

The deer clear the corn on the other side of the field and Alex can hear something else in the woods but can't see anything.

She hears what sounds like a growl but still sees nothing.

She has heard a bear growl, a mountain lion growl, a bobcat growl, a coyote growl, just about every animal she has heard growl and this didn't sound like any of them.

She begins wondering if she is being watched by Bigfoot.

She starts scanning the area more slowly, looking for anything that seems odd, out of place.

She sees a tree that looks like it has something on the side of it that wasn't there earlier.

She watches that spot.

As she is watching that spot it moves.

Her heart stops, at least skips a beat or three.

She can't tell what it is; it is too far to see with her eyes alone. She raises her rifle and uses the scope hoping it will let her see what it is.

As she is getting it into her scope she is hoping to see a bear. But it is larger and then stands upright to walk away. It wasn't looking at her so she doesn't know if it knew she was there or not. She continues to watch it as long as she can as it goes farther from her.

At noon she eats her lunch and continues watching and listening for movement.

About two thirty she hears the unidentified growl again.

She is confused as she never seen or heard the Bigfoot come back.

But then she thinks. The distance it was she shouldn't have been able to hear the growl, at least not as well as she has then or now.

She turns around in her seat to look behind her.

She doesn't see anything on the ground that would look out of place. So she looks up in the trees around her beginning with the ones behind her stand.

What she sees she prays that she didn't see it.

It is the tree behind hers.

No more than fifty feet from her.

She never smelled it either as close as she is, the wind was blowing in its direction all day.

There is no doubt the creature knows she is there. It is staring straight at her.

She has heard horror stories of the creatures kidnapping people and women particularly.

She watches the creature as it watches her.

She reaches down and unsnaps the strap over the pistol in the holster. While watching the creature trying not to let it see her movement. Where the creature is she would never be able to swing the rifle around to get a shot if she needs to, but she could use the pistol.

She doesn't pull the pistol as the creature hasn't given her a reason to be fearful, as yet.

The time she sits there watching the creature seems like hours to her. But it was only ten minutes.

She looks at its face; she is close enough to not need the scope to see the face and the features of the face.

She sees what Joe told her, how human it looks just covered in hair.

She begins to scare herself.

She starts to think, was it there when I came in here? Did it come in after I was here and I didn't hear it? What is it going to do? Will it hurt me? Will I need to defend myself? Could I even shoot it to defend myself? Would I be fast enough to shoot it if it jumps at me? What will it do if I climb down? Will it attack or just watch me? If I leave will it follow me?

The more she thinks the more scared she gets.

She hears a roar that she believes was another Bigfoot. The one she is watching seems to have listened closely. Then it roars, she can feel it and puts her hands over her ears to try to protect her hearing, even if a little.

Before she can re-act, the Bigfoot jumps out of the tree, from a height of approximately twenty feet, and lands on the ground with a loud thud. She even felt the impact in her tree stand. Then it ran into the woods toward the other one that roared. It ran so fast that she had trouble watching it as it went around trees and through the brush.

She decided to give up the hunt for the day and went home. She looked over her shoulder every now and again as she headed to the house to be sure she wasn't being followed.

When she gets to the house Joe asks how the hunt went, and asks if she got one since she is back earlier than usual.

She looks at him and tells him about the Bigfoot in the tree behind her and how she never knew it was there. The wind was blowing toward the Bigfoot and was strong enough she never smelled the creature. She continues telling him how they stared at each other and she could easily see the facial features and how it really does look like a very hairy human and not an ape like face.

Joe listens to her tell about the ordeal as he is working on supper/dinner. It wasn't ready since she came in earlier than her usual time if she hasn't gotten her deer.

Alex decides to help him by setting the table.

Joe stops her as she is reaching into the cabinet to get the plates out for supper. He tells her to put her stuff away and let him do it while she relaxes from her experience.

She gives him a kiss and thanks him. Then hangs up her hunting coat and puts the rifle in the gun safe.

Once she has everything put away she sits down and watches tv until Joe lets her know supper is ready.

They sit down at the table to eat.

Joe asks, "Did you see any deer today?"

Alex, "Yes, all doe."

Joe doesn't want to ask about the Bigfoot she seen. He is curious to know more but wants her to talk about it when she is ready.

They continue eating conversation is small.

Alex asks, "Did you get the corn harvester fixed today?"

Joe, "Almost, just need to finish putting it back together."

Alex, "Nice, so we will be able to use ours for the harvest."

Joe, "Yes."

They finish supper and clear the table.

They wash the dishes and sit down to relax watching tv.

Alex slides in close to Joe. He puts his arm around her.

She doesn't usually slide in against him, at least not in a long time. He figures she must have been more scared than he understood.

Joe just enjoys the moment and doesn't ask about the day hunting.

Alex, "Thank you for holding me tonight."

Joe, "No problem babe; I enjoy moments like this."

She smiles, "I think next time I am taking the 30-06 and leaving the 30-30 home. If I need to shoot Bigfoot I want something with more power behind it."

Joe, "If that is what you want than do it."

They finish watching tv and go to bed.

Chapter 2
The Kill

Again the alarm goes off at four o'clock.

They get up and have breakfast together then Joe gets ready for his day hunting.

Alex makes his lunch while he gets his rifle and other things ready to go.

She notices he has the 44 mag pistol on his belt this morning.

She asks about the pistol.

He tells her it is for extra protection in case needed. Especially after her ordeal; with the Bigfoot behind her and not knowing it was there. He is still carrying his 25-06 rifle.

They kiss and he heads out the door towards his stand.

He is again shining the light side to side as he continues slowly toward his stand.

He is not only concerned about bear, and mountain lion but now Bigfoot as well.

Nobody knows the behavior patterns of Bigfoot. There are theories but that is all they are is theories. Nobody has been able to study them and figure out the different calls and sounds they make. Are they aggressive or not? Many believe they are not aggressive but nobody knows for sure. There are videos and testimonies about their possible aggression, some of it may be misunderstanding of the Bigfoots normal behavior but nobody knows for sure and can't say for sure without the true scientific study of their behavior.

So he continues slowly, watching for any eye shine or the silhouette of a being in his light.

He gets to his tree stand without seeing anything and is relieved.

He shines the light around the area and into the trees close to his stand and again sees nothing.

He climbs into his tree stand relieved nothing is close and he is apparently alone.

As the sun rises he hears noises in the woods and doesn't see anything. Figures it is a squirrel or chipmunk. Perhaps it could be deer moving through the area in the low light of dawn.

After the sun has fully risen he can see the area and can now see the squirrels, chipmunks, and small birds making the noise in the leaves.

He looks in the trees close and as far as he can see, looking for Bigfoot.

He sees nothing and all looks normal to him.

He looks for the dead spike and cannot find it, it isn't laying where he seen it and there is no drag marks to indicate it being removed. The mountain lion and even the bear would have left drag marks, neither one can pick it up high enough to not leave some sort of sign of being removed.

He focuses more on the ground and the known deer trail he is close to.

He hears something but can't see it. So he continues to watch the area the sound is coming from.

He sees a doe come into view.

She is showing signs of being followed, not scared, by stopping and looking behind her.

He hears movement behind the doe. As if it is following her path of travel.

He begins to see brush moving.

He raises his rifle anticipating the arrival of a buck. He is hopeful that it is the buck he is after.

The doe continues walking without showing any fear.

Finally he sees what is following the doe.

It is the ten pointer he was hoping for.

He takes aim.

The buck stops, giving him the perfect shot.

He squeezes the trigger.

The deer jumps as the bullet hits it in the chest.

After the shot the doe runs into the field and continues running.

The buck runs back into the woods where it came from.

Joe gives it ten minutes before he exits his stand to track the deer. Giving it a chance to lay down and die.

Joe doesn't see where the deer laid down. So when he goes over to where it was when he shot to locate the blood trail, he begins the tracking part of his hunt.

He is starting at the point where he shot it because he

couldn't see where it went after being shot. This way he can track the deer and find it so he can take it home to butcher.

He follows the blood trail for a hundred yards maybe a little more and finds the deer laying there already dead.

He is excited as this is the largest buck he has ever gotten. Aside from that it means meat in the freezer this winter.

He looks around before putting his rifle down, making sure there are no large predators in the immediate area.

Once he is sure the bear and mountain lion are not near he leans his rifle against a nearby tree.

Then he takes his tag and his pen and fills in the information and places it onto the ear as required.

He looks around again and verifies he is still alone. He then begins to clean the deer, cutting its belly open to remove the contents saving the heart and liver of the animal.

Once he has it gutted, he ties his drag rope to the deer's neck and begins to drag the almost one hundred fifty pound animal to the field.

Once to the field he looks around and is again satisfied he is still alone and not being stalked by one of the large predators.

He leaves the deer at the edge of the field and goes to the house and gets his pickup and goes back to get the deer.

Alex sees him leave with the pickup and figures he got a deer.

As Joe is approaching the deer he doesn't see anything around the deer.

He pulls up and loads the deer into the back of the pickup then heads to the house.

He pulls into the driveway and Alex walks out to meet him.

He shows her the deer and she is happy knowing they have meat for the freezer and that he got the buck he has been after.

She had already prepared the space in the basement to hang the deer to skin and start cutting the pieces off to process.

They have a large sheet of painter's plastic on the floor and a workbench covered with more plastic to lay the meat on when it is cut off the deer to cut down into pieces.

The meat grinder is attached to the workbench with a stainless steel pan on chair to catch the ground meat.

They do not mix their meat with pork or beef like some folks do to add the fat that the deer is missing. Another reason they butcher their own deer.

The rear quarters are cut down into chunks to go through the grinder for Hamburg and they save some as stew meat for soup.

The front quarters are where they cut their steaks from. Yeah the steaks are smaller but they prefer to have more Hamburg meat.

They cut one side of the ribs for bar-b-q ribs, confident Alex will get her deer for at least one more side of ribs. They cut the neck for a roast as they finish butchering the deer.

They have a friend that will take the hide of the deer and process it, tan, to sell.

They finish processing the deer and package the meat into freezer bags then place the meat in the freezer. They label the bags as deer and the month and year, so they use the older meat first.

Joe shot his deer about eight o'clock in the morning and it is now one o'clock in the afternoon. They have butchered enough and have gotten a system when they butcher that allows them to be more efficient when butchering without it taking most of the day. Another reason Alex makes sure everything is ready before the deer is even shot.

They clean up the area and sharpen the knives before placing them on the workbench for the next deer.

They have a quick lunch, sandwiches, and then Joe goes to the shed and works on the harvester trying to get it done that day.

They don't have a large combine for their corn harvest. They still use a small harvester attachment for their tractor.

They would love to get a combine, but the money isn't available even for a used one at this time.

Alex does the evening milking of the cow so Joe can focus on finishing the harvester.

Alex has supper almost complete by the time Joe comes in from working on the harvester.

Joe gets cleaned up, washing his hands, arms and face before supper.

Joe sets the table while Alex finishes cooking.

Alex sets the food on the table and they sit down to eat.

Joe asks, "How much bologna do we want to make this year?"

Alex shrugs her shoulders, "Suppose that depends on how much we will give to the kids."

Joe smiles, "They do enjoy the venison bologna."

Alex smiles in return, "Most people do."

Joe thinks while eating. "How about we take the ribs from your deer and we make the rest of it into bologna?"

Alex looks at him, "Suppose that could work. You don't want any more steaks or Hamburger from my deer?"

Joe considers her question for a short time. "No, I think I'd prefer bologna over more Hamburger and steaks."

Alex, "Well I guess the only thing left is for me to get a deer."

They both smile and they finish their meal.

While they are washing the dishes Alex speaks up. "At least with the bologna will we get to see the kids and grandkids when they come to get some of it."

Joe smiles, "That is the idea my dear."

They finish the dishes and sit down to watch tv like most nights.

Alex is silently thinking about her day hunting tomorrow.

She is excited to go out but scared at the same time.

She knows she will be heavily armed and will be able to protect herself if needed. But there is the unknown about the Bigfoot that scares her.

They go to bed and get up with the alarm in the morning.

Joe asked her how she slept. He noticed she did more tossing and turning during the night than usual, but doesn't tell her.

She says she slept decent, not great but acceptable.

Joe looks at her and doesn't say anything about her keeping him up most of the night.

He couldn't understand her mumbling in her sleep, so he has nothing to ask about.

They have breakfast and she gets ready to hunt and he gets ready for the morning chores.

A cold system moved into the area and so they dressed a bit warmer than they have been.

Since she expected to be sitting in a stand all day she wore thermal underwear and winter hunting coat with pants. She also wore an orange knit hat that was a ski mask for the cold.

Joe wore his heavy work coat with pants minus the thermal underwear since he wasn't planning on being in the cold all day. He could go inside to warm up as needed.

Before Alex walked out the door she double checked that she had the correct rifle and a full box of ammo. The pistol and a box of ammo, as well as everything she needs to tag, clean and drag her deer.

As Alex walked to her stand she waved the light back and forth and walked slower than usual.

She stopped and loaded the pistol after leaving the house.

She wants to have something to protect herself with; if needed.

The pistol is in its holster but the strap to hold it in isn't snapped, for quicker access if needed.

She is more aware of every sound and is questioning sounds that she never questioned before.

She wants to believe that she is being paranoid and over thinking the whole issue with Bigfoot. But then she remembers the accounts of Bigfoot being aggressive and she wants to give the creature the benefit of the doubt. But yet she doesn't want to trust that which shouldn't be trusted without it showing it can be trusted.

She isn't afraid of bears or mountain lions. She knows she is part of their food chain and she understands their behavior well enough to know when she needs to re-act and if she may need to kill the predator. So far to date she has been able to avoid killing a bear out of season and hasn't had a mountain lion approach as close as Joe has had them.

She gets to her stand and shines the light into the tree that the Bigfoot was in a couple days ago and it is empty. She shines the light around the area and into every tree the light can reach and can find nothing to be concerned about, not even any eye shine.
She climbs into her tree stand and gets settled in her seat for the day.

As dawn breaks she hears movement in the forest in the dry leaves.

She assumes it is squirrels or perhaps chipmunks, maybe even deer moving through in the low light to avoid being seen.

She tracks the sound into the corn field and can hear it going through the corn.

She realizes it is a big animal like deer or bear. So she continues to listen to the movement of the animal as the sun rises and she can see more of the area.

The sun is high enough and the area is lit well enough that she can see what is around.

She sees nothing inside the tree line and she looks in the surrounding trees and sees nothing other than a squirrel that decided to come out of its nest.

She focuses on the corn where she hears the noise of a large animal through the standing corn stalks. Moving the stalks as it goes through, she is high enough in her tree stand to see the corn stalks moving.

She double checks that she loaded the rifle and that the pistol is secured in the holster.

She sits ready as it sounds like and looks like the animal is coming towards her through the corn.

The animal comes out of the corn and is the bear.

She is relieved it is not Bigfoot.

Although the bear is sniffing the air; as if it can smell something.

She knows it isn't her as the wind is coming to her from the bear.

She watches the bear and takes note of the direction it is focusing its attention.

The bear is staring into the woods past her.

She gives quick glances in the direction the bear is staring but sees nothing and doesn't want to ignore the bear too long. The bear is close and if she takes her attention and focuses it into the woods where the bear is looking, the bear could surprise her by climbing her tree becoming a real threat.

The bear walks towards the road and away from her and the area it was staring into.

She watches the bear and she gives quick glances in the direction the bear was staring.

The bear crosses the road and looks to be heading in the direction of Joes stand on the other side of the farm.

She turns her attention to the woods where the bear was focused.

She still sees nothing. She does notice that it is quiet. No birds singing, no squirrels or chipmunks moving around or chattering.

She understands that usually means a large predator is in the area.

The bear left and her presence didn't seem to bother the animal so she wonders what is out there that she can't see.

She begins thinking about the mountain lion. It would be

able to lay low enough in the underbrush that she wouldn't see it. But then she is confused why the bear chose to avoid it altogether.

So now she thinks it could be a larger bear. It would still be able to hide in the brush to the point she wouldn't be able to see it. She looks around and not just in that area, still hoping that a buck comes her way today.

She is hoping that the bear didn't scare the deer away for the day.

The small animals start to come out of hiding again and she starts to feel some relieve at that time. Because if the small animals are feeling safe; than perhaps the deer will feel safe enough to come out as well.

As noon approaches she hears something coming through the woods. It is moving fast by the sounds of it.

She watches and four doe come into her line of sight and continue running into the corn field.

She watches in the direction the deer came from and sees nothing. She is sure something was chasing the deer but still sees nothing and cannot hear anything in the woods.

Again all went quiet.

She is convinced there is something out there just beyond where she can see clearly.

She focuses on the area the deer came from and thinks she sees something move.

She raises her rifle and uses the scope to look at what she saw moving.

All she can make out is a large animal, dark in color, low to the ground. It doesn't seem to look like a mountain lion, the only bear they know of on the farm left, unless it circled back around.

She is confused as to what it might be, she figures the bear must have circled back into the woods where she couldn't see it and scared the deer.

She remembers the bear was focused on that area and is wondering if a larger bear did move into the area.

She lowers her rifle and continues to watch that area as she watches around her as well still hoping for a buck to appear.

The time keeps slipping away on her, as it does to us all, and it is now going on three o'clock.

She hears something in the corn field and turns to watch and wait.

Her patience pays off as a six point buck walks out of the corn and stops.

He is not broad side for the perfect shot but he is positioned well enough for a good shot.

The buck looks away from her and she raises her rifle and takes aim at his front shoulder.

Before she can release the safety the deer runs to the far end of the field.

She is confused as to what would have scared the deer to run like that. But no matter the deer is still within range and is positioned for a good shot anyway.

She raises the rifle again and finds the deer in the scope and gets the shot off this time.

She sees it drop in her scope and gets excited, meat for the freezer.

When she lowers the rifle she sees the deer running through the woods.

Now she is confused, is it the same deer?

She stays in her stand and can see body.

She watches it and is praying she didn't shoot a doe that she didn't know was there.

After ten minutes of no movement from the body she climbs out of her stand and walks over to it slowly. So if it isn't completely dead it can get up and run off without hurting her.

When she gets to the body she can't believe what she is seeing. Granted the smell is a giveaway as well.

She has confirmed killing a Bigfoot.

Granted it was mistaken identity as she thought she was seeing the deer in her scope.

She stays back and throws a stone and hits it in the head. The creature doesn't move; she can see no signs of it breathing. She sees where the bullet hit it in the chest right where she believes the heart to be.

She begins to freak out, realizing she shot Bigfoot.

She runs for the house. She doesn't stop until she gets inside.

Joe looks at her. "I heard you shoot; I suspect you got it since you're here now and out of breath."

She looks at him, "Get the truck and take me back there, you ain't gonna believe it if I tell you."

She tells him to grab his 44 mag as well.

He looks at her, "Why would I need that?"

Alex, "Don't question, just do it and let's go."

Joe grabs the 44 mag pistol from the gun safe and they get in the truck and go to her stand.

Joe, "So where is it?"

Alex points to the far end of the field.

They drive up to the end of the field and Joe sees the body from a distance.

Joe, "Wow that is a large deer."

Alex smiles and says nothing.

They get to the body and Joe sees exactly what it is.

Joe is amazed and in disbelieve. "Oh my, you shot a Bigfoot."

Alex, "Look at the hair color. I thought I was sighting in on the deer that stood here."

Joe, "The hair color does resemble a deer's color."

Alex, "Well let's get it loaded up and go see what we can do with it. There has to be someone that wants it for study."

Joe, "I am sure there are a lot of somebodies that would love to have it for study. But the question is how to find them and how long will it take for them to get here."

They get out of the truck and get the creature positioned at the tail gate and they work together to load it into the back of the truck.

Joe mentions how it seems to be heavier than the bear he shot a couple years ago. He mentions the bear was almost five hundred pounds and this feels heavier.

Alex, "I agree but we need to get this loaded. This isn't the one that was behind me the other day."

Joe looks at her, "You mean there is another one?"

Alex, "Yes, is this the color of the one you saw?"

Joe, "No, The one I saw was darker."

They get it loaded and as they are getting in the truck they hear one roar.

It doesn't sound close but they definitely take notice to the roar.

Joe follows the road around the edge of the corn back to the road and they return to the house.

Alex, "Where are you going to park the truck for the night? I doubt anyone will be able to come get it tonight."

Joe, "You don't think it would be ok just sitting out like usual?"

Alex, "There is a reason no remains have been found. If the others take the dead and bury them or the scavengers eat the dead nobody knows."

Alex stands with the rifle at the ready as Joe parks the truck in the shed and closes the doors for the night.

Alex points to the area for a lock.

Joe gives her a confused look, "Really?"

Alex staying serious and using her mommy voice, "Yes really, lock it."

Joe locks the doors and they go inside.

As they get to the door they hear a Bigfoot roar. It sounds like it is in the area of her stand beside the corn.

They stop and look in that direction and can't see anything.

They hear another roar from the same area, louder and somehow different.

They listen as it roars again, the same sound in its voice.

Alex looks at Joe, "It sounds sad, like it is morning the loss of the one in the shed."

Joe agrees and listen to it roar again.

Then they hear more Bigfoot all around the property return the call with the same mournful tone.

They look at each other and get inside without saying another word.

They can't hear the calls inside the house and are relieved but concerned at the same time, because now they can't track the movement of the creatures.

Chapter 3
The Search

They sit down to eat supper that night. Listening to sounds outside.

They don't talk much at all during supper and just listen.

Alex, more than Joe, is convinced that the remaining Bigfoot will be looking for the dead one.

After supper they wash the dishes then Joe sits down at the computer looking for Bigfoot hunters, scientists and pretty much anyone that would want the creature for scientific study.

Alex is listening to the sounds outside and is very jumpy.

The dogs look at the door and growl at one point.

She looks out the window and sees a barn cat running across the yard toward the barn. She figures the dogs were growling at the sounds of the cat outside the door.

Joe asks if she can remember any names of any of the hunters that they have seen on tv looking for Bigfoot.

She says no, "But there is the college professor out west that studies Bigfoot and is considered an expert. Perhaps you can find him and maybe he can direct you to someone to take the creature."

Joe looks for the professor and finds one and calls the number that is associated to the name he finds.

Joe leaves a message and then emails the professor as well and includes his number so hopefully the professor will call tonight.

Joe keeps looking online for anyone in the Bigfoot hunting world that he can get in touch with tonight.

His cell phone begins ringing and the number is from Utah so he answers it hoping it is the professor.

Joe, "Hello."

Jay, "Hello, my name is Jay Rockington. I received your message and your email to call you about a Bigfoot."

Joe, "Yes, Thank you for calling tonight."

Jay, "I don't think I completely understand what you are looking for from me. I don't actively hunt Bigfoot. People bring the evidence to me and I study that to determine real or fake. But it sounded like you said you have killed one."

Joe, "Actually sir, my wife killed it, accidently."

Jay, "That is interesting, how did she accidently kill it?"

Joe, "The hair color is light and she thought she was sighting in on the deer she saw in that area, it was on all fours and she shot it believing it was the deer, until walking up to it."

Jay, "Wait you say it has light hair color?"

Joe, "Yes, is that significant?'

Jay, "I am not sure, you see most people talk about dark colored hair not light enough to be mistaken for a deer."

Joe, "I understand that. Did you get the attachment I sent in the email? It is a picture of the Bigfoot in the back of my truck."

Jay, "Yes, I did get it, and it is very interesting. But remember I have seen pictures similar to yours that were fakes, not saying yours is a fake. So what is it that you are looking to do with the Bigfoot?"

Joe, "We are wanting to get rid of it as soon as possible. Preferably to someone like yourself that wants it for scientific study and not to hide it from the public. Like most suspect the government would do."

Jay, "Well you say in your email you are in Pa?"

Joe, "Yes."

Jay, "Well I couldn't get there for a couple days at least. But I may know someone closer to you. Let me call them and see if she will take it off your hands, so to speak. I must tell you there is no guarantee of money for the Bigfoot."

Joe, "That is fine, if we were interested in getting paid for it we would look for someone that is offering money for one. I saw some of them while searching for you."

They end their conversation and Jay tells Joe that if his contact is interested it will be a call from a New Jersey number. Joe acknowledges that and they end the call.

Their entire call was pleasant and even though Jay never mentioned it he could hear the sincerity in Joe's voice and therefor decided to believe him.

Alex hears the cows in the pasture sounding excited, not in a good way. More like when coyotes are in the pasture with them.

Alex excitedly asks, "So what did he say? Does he want the Bigfoot or not?"

Joe staying calm, "He is calling a friend of his who is in Jersey and hopefully we will be getting a call from her tonight."

Alex, "Did you say her? We will be getting a call from a her? Or rather you will get the call."

Joe looks at her, surprised that she would even consider getting jealous let alone actually verbalizing it to him, even if unintentional.

Joe, "Yes I said it will be a woman that will call about the Bigfoot in the shed. Jay said he wouldn't be able to get here for a couple days and that his friend is in Jersey and will decide if she wants it or not."

Alex, "Did he mention about money?"

Joe, "Yes he did, and he can't guarantee money for the Bigfoot."

Alex looks a little depressed, "Did he say why?"

Joe, "No babe he didn't and I didn't ask. I would suspect they would need to verify the thing is real first. He did say he has seen pictures of fake ones in the back of pickup trucks before."

Alex, "Makes sense, but hopefully we can get something out of it, financially speaking."

Joe agrees that would be nice but mentions to not expect it.

Joe's cell phone rings and he sees the number is listed as New Jersey so he answers it.

Joe is curious to see if it is the person Jay was going to have call, "Hello."

The female voice has a heavy Mexican accent, "Hello, my name is Juanita. My friend, Jay, tell me call you. That you have Bigfoot dead and want it gone."

Joe is relieved it sounds like this is the person he was waiting for. "Yes ma'am."

Juanita, "Ok, You have picture you can send?"

Joe, "Yes, is this your cell number? I can send the picture in a text message."

Juanita, "Yes, that is good. I call back after I see picture."

Joe, "Ok I will send it right away."

They end their call and Joe sends the picture in a text message to her.

Joe and Alex are quietly waiting for the return call.

They hear the cows sounding agitated. Like something is in the pasture with them of the predator nature.

Alex keeps Joe's phone while he grabs his 25-06 from the gun safe and goes outside looking around with a rechargeable spotlight.

He doesn't see anything other than the cows.

He does notice they are all together in a group like a predator is around, but he doesn't see anything to be concerned about.

He shines the light around the yard and around the shed where his pickup is parked with the Bigfoot in the back and again sees nothing.

He figures it must be coyotes because anything larger he would have been able to see. The coyotes have learned to hide behind the cattle when they group together, but usually the coyotes run off when he comes out looking. So it is difficult, at best, to see the coyotes with the cows at night.

He is satisfied that whatever had the cows agitated has moved on so he goes back inside.

As he is putting the rifle away his cell phone rings.

Alex hands it to him and he answers it.

Joe sees the number is New Jersey again, "Hello."

Juanita, "Mr. Mason?"

Joe, "Yes."

Juanita, "Oh good, I got right number this time. Some reason phone call wrong number before. I look at the picture you send. The hair is wrong color. Is too light color, not dark enough to be Bigfoot. Are you sure light was good when take picture?"

Joe, "Yes ma'am; light was good and that is the color of the hair, no tricks of lighting or camera."

Juanita, "This is very odd color indeed. They usually darker. How big is Bigfoot you have?"

Joe, "My wife and I estimated it to be about eight and a half feet tall. We guess eight hundred pounds, roughly. We have not measured or weighed it."

Juanita, "Ok, sometime hard to weigh the Bigfoot."

Joe, "Yes we do not have a scale big enough to weigh the Bigfoot."

Juanita, "Where you have the Bigfoot now?"

Joe, "It is in the back of the pickup wrapped in a tarp and parked inside the shed."

Juanita, "You do good. Do you see or hear anything outside after having Bigfoot dead at house?"

Joe, "The cows are restless. I figure the coyotes are back in the area at least that is how the cows are acting."

Juanita, "Did you or you wife see different Bigfoot. Not the one is dead, but different one?"

Joe, "Yes, we both saw at least one that had much darker hair."

Juanita is silent for a little while she thinks and Joe looks at his phone to see if they are still connected.

Joe asks if she is still there.

Juanita answers, "Yes; I still here. I thinking, you dead Bigfoot is big enough to be adult, but color is odd. Not dark enough to be adult, but young are usually dark also."

Joe, "Yes my wife actually thought it was the deer she saw there when she shot it. The hair color is that close to the deer."

Juanita, "I wish to come see the Bigfoot. May I come tomorrow?"

Joe, "Yes, please come tomorrow."

Joe gives her the address and tells her that the GPS in her phone will lead her straight to the house.

Juanita thanks him and tells him to be careful. Because nobody knows how the other Bigfoots will re-act to having one killed. She mentions that to her knowledge no one has ever killed one to know how they will re-act.

He thanks her and they end the call.

He tells Alex about the discussion and about the warning.

Alex, "She is definitely coming tomorrow?"

Joe, "That is what she said."

They settle down to watch their favorite shows on tv.

A few minutes into their show the dogs start barking and growling at the door.

Joe gets up to let the dogs out but when he opens the door the dogs run away from the door and to Alex.

They both figure that is strange behavior for the dogs. They have never ran away from the door before, not even when the bear was in the yard. The dogs chased it out of the yard.

Joe grabs the spot light and steps outside and shines the light around.

He thinks he saw movement but while he held the light on that area there was no movement.

He goes back inside and hangs the spotlight on its recharging station and returns to the couch to watch tv with Alex.

After a few minutes go by the two dogs split and go to separate windows and start growling.

The German Shepard is at the window closer to Alex and the Husky is at the window at the opposite end of the room.

The hair on the dogs back is standing up and they are both growling with teeth showing at the window they face.

Joe goes and gets the spotlight again and shines it out the windows, one at a time, and sees nothing. He even walks over to each window and shines the light out the window and still sees nothing.

He looks at the dogs and tells them to lay down and calls them dumb dogs, growling at nothing what is wrong with you?

They are sitting and watching tv and every so often one of the dogs look up and gives a low growl at a window.

The dogs are staying with Joe and Alex and not leaving either of them out of site.

There is a crashing sound on the back porch and both dogs run barking and growling.

Joe and Alex jumped at the sound as well.

Joe goes to look outside and sees the metal trash cans knocked over with the contents spilled out of the can. The tight fitting lids are off and in the yard.

The cans that were knocked over has the chicken feed in one, cat food in another and the third has the dog food in it.

Neither can is light. All three were full; they were just filled that morning.

He is thinking out loud, "Now the raccoons never knocked those over before."

He goes out to clean up the mess.

He shines the light around and sees nothing.

Both dogs are with him and they are aggressively growling and barking into the darkness behind Joe.

Each time he shines the light to see what the dogs see there is nothing to be seen.

As he is cleaning the last bit of chicken food up off the porch he catches wind of a foul odor.

He looks at the dogs and asks them which one farted.

Joe fanning his hand in front of his face, "Oh man one of you stink; I hope you don't fart like that in the house you stinky dogs."

Before going back inside Joe tells the dogs to go potty.

The dogs look at him, look at each other and leave the porch.

They don't go far from the porch and while one is doing its business the other watches the dark. One of them is always on guard that night.

Joe takes the dogs back inside hoping that they took care of business outside and won't be stinking up the house with their farting.

They get inside and Joe goes and sits beside Alex.

Alex moves away from and him and holds her nose, "What was out there a skunk? Because you stink honey."

Joe sniffs himself, "No the dogs farted and they were up wind of me so I got to smell it and apparently wear the smell as well."

Alex shakes her head, "Honey you smell more like the Bigfoot than a dog fart."

Joe looks at her, "Oh snot head, I wonder if that is what the dogs are growling at tonight."

Alex looks at him wide eyed, "You think those creatures are here……….tonight?" As she is looking out each window as fast as she can turn her head.

Joe sees the idea of the creature being outside is disturbing her. Perhaps even scarring her, he is leaning more towards her being scared.

Joe goes to the gun safe and grabs the 357 and the 44 pistols and goes back to her and hands her the 357 and a box of ammo.

Joe, "In case we need them, and if nothing else piece of mind tonight."

Alex smiles as she takes the pistol.

Alex, "Thank you."

Joe smiles, "Welcome."

They sit there and load the pistols.

Both pistols are revolvers.

Once they are loaded they place the pistols back in there holster and snap the securement strap behind the hammer, to help prevent accidental discharge from snagging the hammer on anything that could pull it back and release it onto a live round.

They hear a load crash out back again.

They both go and look.

They step outside with the spotlight and see all three cans of food in the yard.

The content of each is strewn across the yard and the cans are destroyed, smashed beyond using anymore. They don't even see the lids to any of the cans.

Joe and Alex look at each other.

Joe, "Those cans are not light especially when I just filled them today."

Alex, "I know; I can barely lift them by myself. There is at least one hundred pounds of food in each one of those cans, or there was."

Joe is still shining the light around the area looking for anything that doesn't look right.

Movement, a shadow that doesn't seem to fit anything, that seems out of place.

He notices the cows are still huddled together in a defensive group. So he figures whatever is around is still there.

So he moves the light slowly around the area, trying to see anything out of place.

He is expecting to see the bear, even praying to see the bear. At least he would have a better idea of the behavior to expect.

Alex points out a motion light that is on near the barns exterior. On the side, that there should be no movement.

Joe reaches down and unsnaps the strap over his 44 revolver and he begins to walk towards the barn. He tells Alex to take the dogs inside before he walks away from the house.

Once he starts walking away he pulls the revolver out of the holster.

Alex lets the dogs in and follows Joe.

He doesn't realize she is behind him.

He is moving slowly and quietly.

He pauses to listen and hears movement behind him. He turns and sees Alex.

Joe is not pleased and lets her know, "Dang girl, I could have shot you. I didn't know you were following me. I thought you went inside with the dogs."

Alex, "I didn't want you out here alone. Besides I know you would take the time to see what was behind you before shooting. I wouldn't put that trust in just anybody."

Joe shakes his head, "Thank you babe, but I wish you would have let me know you were going to follow me."

Alex smiles, knowing that goes a long way with him and the right smile gets her out of trouble easier.

He turns and again walks slowly toward the barn, with Alex

beside him.

Alex as well has her pistol in hand and not holstered.

The motion light goes out before they get to the area its sensors are aimed to read.

They look at each other knowing that whatever it was has either left the area or is no longer moving.

Joe is praying quietly that the critter, whatever it was, has moved on.

They get closer and keep shining the spot light in that direction as well as the surrounding area trying to see anything that would be in the area.

They reach the area of the barn where the motion light sensor reaches and the light comes on.

They see nothing in the area of the light.

Joe moves the spot light to light up the shadowy areas the motion light won't light up.

Alex is looking at the doors to the barn and notices the doors are not completely closed like they usually are for the night.

Joe notices something moving in the tall grass that doesn't get mowed all summer between the field and the driveway across from the front of the barn.

Joe goes to get Alex's attention at the same time she tries to get his.

They look at each other and point so the other can see what they saw.

Alex grabs Joe's arm that has the light.

She moves his arm to re-aim the light.

He looks where she is aiming the light and they see eye shine and the outline of something human shaped but yet larger.

Joe is not sure what to think, "Hey, you in the tall grass. We see you and you are trespassing and need to leave here immediately. We both have firearms and will not hesitate to use them."

The being doesn't move; acting like it hasn't been seen.

Alex looks at the barn doors and notices something looking out at them.

She nudges Joe and points to the barn doors, "Do you see what I see?"

Joe looks at the doors, "Do you see someone, something starring at us?"

Alex with a shaky scared voice, "Yes, do you?"

Joe with a similar voice, "Yes, I think we need to get back to the house. We have seen two, how many do we not see?"

Alex still scared voice, "I wish you wouldn't have said that out loud."

Joe smiles, "You were thinking it as well."

Alex, "Yes I was, but it didn't need to be said out loud."

It is in that time frame that the wind shifts and they smell the odor of the creature.

They also notice tracks in the loose dirt in the driveway.

Large human like shoeless foot prints in the loose dirt.

Alex keeps looking at the creatures, shifting her gaze from one to the other, "You shoot the one in the barn since you have the more powerful pistol and have a better chance at a kill shot if you shoot through the door. I'll shoot the one in the grass and then we can get to the house."

Joe shakes his head, "Babe, you have a good idea. The problem is how many do we not see? If we shoot these two and get fortunate enough to kill both of them, how many come out of the dark before we get to the house? We need to have a better idea of how many are here before we shoot any of them. We don't know if they are here for the dead one or something else, and we definitely have no idea how many are here."

Alex looks at him, "I hate you. I hate it when you make sense."

Joe smiles, "And I love you as well babe."

They start walking slowly back to the house. Watching in front of themselves, and behind as they walk. Keeping the light; and their heads; on swivels.

Chapter 4
A Long Night

They make it back to the house and as they go onto the porch they hear a Bigfoot roar and it is closer than they wanted to know by how load it was.

They felt the roar in their bodies.

They had to cover their ears it was so loud.

They get inside and hear more Bigfoot's roar and even howl.

They are so loud the windows in the house are shaking (rattling).

They even notice some objects on the selves bouncing to the sound of the creatures.

Joe and Alex open the gun safe and begin loading every firearm they have.

They load the shotguns and the rifles and keep their pistols with them.

Both dogs are trying to hide from not only the creatures but the deafening sounds the creatures are making as well.

Joe and Alex turn off all the lights in the house so they can see out easier than the creature can see in.

They hear something hit the side of the house at the front door area.

Alex investigates and sees nothing.

Another hit opposite side of the house.

Joe investigates and sees nothing.

Another hit at the back door.

Joe investigates and again sees nothing.

Joe joins up with Alex in the living room.

Joe continues watching windows, "Babe, I don't think that is just one creature, do you?"

Alex is scanning the windows as well, "No I don't hun."

They hear glass break upstairs.

Joe runs up to see what happened and Alex stays on the first floor.

Joe finds a window broken in one of the spare rooms.

He looks around without turning on the light and sees a large rock on the floor.

He looks at the rock and knows the size of it is heavier than a normal human can throw. He believes there are humans that could throw it but none that he knows. And he isn't sure that even those humans could throw it the height to reach the second floor.

He totally believes it was thrown by a Bigfoot.

He makes sure the room across the hall is empty and that the creature is not in there then he stands back in the doorway of that room across the hall from that one with the rock and watches to see if there is any movement in that room. They never heard any movement upstairs and so he believes it never came in or it hasn't left that room.

He hears movement but can't tell for sure if it is in the room or outside on the porch roof.

He continues watching the room and he can see the broken window.

He watches with rifle ready if he sees a creature inside or at the window.

He never sees what he was hearing moving around.

The sound of movement has stopped and he isn't sure what to think.

Is it inside? Is it still on the roof? Is it safe to move from that spot and check on Alex?

The Husky comes up the stairs without the German Shepard.

The dog looks at Joe and looks across the hall to the other room and growls.

The dog joins Joe in the room and lays beside him.

Joe has moved a chair into position so he can sit and watch the room. Since he has no idea how long he will need to be there to watch the window and room.

He asks the dog where the other dog is and it looks downstairs so he figures the other dog stayed with Alex.

There is more Bigfoot roars, howls; whistles and other noises that they figure are from the creatures.

Joe is thinking that the creature or creatures at the house are distracting them from seeing what the others are doing outside.

Joe takes his cell phone and texts Alex what he is thinking. He looks up every so often to watch the room and the window. Knowing he could easily miss a creature crossing the window or entering through the broken window.

Bigfoot's Revenge

Alex has her phone on silent mode and it vibrates when Joe's text comes in.

She reads it and sends back that she agrees they are being distracted.

He also has his phone on silent mode and after reading her message he sends back asking if she has seen anything.

She responds with a no and asks what broke upstairs and if he has seen anything.

He lets her know a window in their son's old room had a rock thrown through it and he has been watching that window and room since finding it.

She asks if the Husky found him and he lets her know the dog found him and asks if the other dog is with her, she admits the dog is with her.

He lets her know that the dog growls at the room every so often. It isn't constant and not always loud.

She asks if he wants her and the other dog to come up.

He tells her to come on up.

Alex and the German Shepard get to Joe and join him in the room.

The German Shepard joins the Husky at growling at the other room.

Neither dog; will go into the room and they are not being loud or very aggressive with their growling.

Joe whispers to Alex that he is going to go over and check the room to see if he can see anything inside.

Alex tells him to be careful and she has his back.

Joe walks across the hallway and to the doorway.

He looks around the room and sees nothing that shouldn't be there in the dark.

He looks at the bed and tries to see if something has tried to hide under the bed. Something that would be too big to fit under the bed.

But the bed seems to be normal as well.

He can smell the creature but the odor is not strong. So he figures it must not be inside because the odor would be stronger and more obvious.

He looks at the closet before going on into the room as well and the door is still closed.

He enters the room, moving towards the window.

Alex gives the dogs the hand signal to stay and she moves to the doorway of the room Joe is in.

Joe gets to the window and gets against the wall to see outside the window as best as he can without sticking his head out the window.

The creature's odor is stronger at the window but not over powering like Joe would have expected.

Joe gets down on the floor and crawls, staying lower than the window sill, to the other side of the window before standing up again.

He looks out the window again trying to see as close to the house as he can without sticking his head out the window.

He is able to see something out of the ordinary but can't say for sure that it is a Bigfoot.

He can't see the entire creature. If it is the creature and not something they threw against the house that stuck to the wall.

Alex is still at the door and sees Joe motion with hand signals he sees something outside.

They hear a noise downstairs.

Joe looks at Alex and she points to herself and then downstairs letting Joe know she will go check it out.

Joe nods his acknowledgement and agreeance.

Alex heads downstairs and the German Shepard follows and the Husky stays upstairs with Joe.

The dog follows Alex staying behind her as they go down the stairs.

Alex is moving slowly and the dog matches her speed, stopping when she stops.

They get to the bottom of the stairs and they all hear a Bigfoot roar.

It is loud enough, again, to rattle the windows in the frames and they can feel it vibrate the floor they stand on.

She knows it is close but she doesn't see it and wonders if it is just outside the door.

She begins asking herself question, quietly in her head.

Has it tried to get in?

Is one already in the house?

She didn't lower the rifle as the creature roared.

She did, however, wince at the sound and wanted to cover her ears.

She scans the living room and she can see it looks normal.

She moves towards the kitchen slowly keeping the rifle at the ready.

She stands against the wall next to the doorway into the kitchen and looks around one side of the kitchen.

She sees nothing and quickly moves to the side of the doorway and looks around the other half of the kitchen.

Again she sees nothing obvious.

Her dog stayed on the other side of the doorway where she first stood.

She looks at the dog and the dog appears to be calm.

She moves into the kitchen, again, keeping the rifle at the ready.

The dog follows her, staying behind her as they walk around the kitchen.

She stays away from the windows but looks out through the windows into the night trying to see what is out there and where it is.

Her hope by staying back away from the windows is that she will blend in with the darkness inside and, at the least, be harder to see.

By counter on the floor she notices broken glass reflecting the light coming in the window from outside.

It was a family picture of her, Joe, the kids, the kids' spouses and grandkids.

She doesn't approach the area, not knowing exactly how it fell from the nail it hung on.

She continues to look around the first floor of the house and that is the only thing she notices out of place.

She doesn't go into the basement.

Joe is still upstairs watching that area outside and it hasn't moved. He can't even tell if it is breathing.

Alex and the dog return to Joe and he motions to her to check the next room.

She walks over to the next room and checks it one side at a time like she did downstairs.

She sees something on the wall, next to the window but can't see exactly what it is.

She knows that her daughter left nothing there and neither, Joe or herself has hung anything in the room.

Once she is certain the room is free from the possibility of a creature she walks in, slowly keeping her guard up.

The dog follows her and gives no warning signals of anything wrong.

They all hear more sounds from the Bigfoots outside. Everything from the house shaking roar to a simple whistle.

Alex gets to the wall and checks out the window by staying against the wall on each side of the window.

She can see the object that Joe sees from his window.

She isn't sure what it is either by looking through the window.

She is sure there is no creature outside of the window so she moves to what she saw inside on the wall.

She can see where something has penetrated the wall from outside. But it hasn't come all the way through the wall. What she is able to see inside is where the wall started to give way to allow the object inside but the wall held together enough to not give up the identity of the object.

She wants to open the window to look out and see what it is for sure but knows the risk is too high and it could be the last mistake she makes.

So she goes back to the opposite side of the window trying to get a better look at what it might be.

As she is looking and trying to see the object better the dog starts growling at the window she is next to.

She stands still and watches the dog and listens to the dogs vocal changes in the growling, becoming more aggressive.

She knows something is there even though she can't see it her dog either hears it or smells it or possibly both.

She can't smell anything with the window closed.

She isn't hearing anything moving outside either but she trusts her dog and stays alert.

Over in the next room Joe's dog is also growling and is getting more aggressive as well.

Joe can smell the creature and can hear movement outside.

The sound of movement isn't loud so he isn't sure if that means it isn't close or if it means it is moving slowly and intentionally trying to be quiet.

The smell isn't over powering either. The odor is stronger than when he first walked into the room but not strong enough to indicate the creature is close.

He as well trusts the dog and stays alert.
Joe notices the odor getting stronger, to the point he wants to cover his nose.

He figures the creature must be close but where, he can't see it.

Alex can smell the creature now with the window closed and she is thinking like Joe. Where is it, it must be close but I can't see it.

Both Joe and Alex are staying out of the window. Staying to one side of the window.

They are both looking at the object that is against the outside wall.

Both dogs stand and are now aggressively growling at the window.

All of a sudden a creature appears on the porch roof.

It apparently jumped from the ground onto the roof landing on all fours and stays crouched on all fours looking at the windows. It focuses in on Joe's window more as the window is broken and it must be able to hear the Husky growling easier than the German Shepard through a closed window.

Alex is watching the creature and sees it focus on Joe's window.

She is hoping that Joe is still looking in that direction and sees the creature.

She also knows that Joe will not reveal himself for the shot as long as the creature is looking in his direction.

Joe does see the creature and is waiting to see what it does.

If it comes at the window he will step out and take the shot. Otherwise he will wait until it looks away from his window.

The creature is still on all fours starring at the window.

It isn't as concerned with Alex's window, probably because it is closed and that it is easier to hear the dog growling through the broken window.

That is what Joe is thinking for the reasoning.

He figures the German Shepard is growling as well but must be harder to hear.

Joe is not standing in a way that he can take the shot without moving.

He must wait until the creature gives him the chance to move without being seen.

Joe gets the Husky to quiet down by using hand signals. The dog is still growling but just not as loud.

The Bigfoot seems to notice the change in the volume coming from the windows and turns its focus on the window Alex is next to.

Joe and Alex both get really good looks at the face of the Bigfoot and have no doubt it is the same creature they saw in the woods while hunting. It may not be the exact same individual, but definitely the same species, at the least.

Alex is as focused on the Bigfoot as it is on her window.

She is standing in a way that she can take the shot, but doesn't want to shoot through the glass of the window.

Joe uses the time to reposition himself for a shot.

He is right handed and had his right shoulder against the wall. He is now able to reposition himself away from the wall enough to get the rifle and himself into a shooting position.

The Bigfoot slowly approaches the object stuck to the wall, staying on all fours seemingly trying not to be noticed.

Joe estimates this one is at least the same size and approximate weight as the dead one. But it is staying low and is hard to estimate. So he figures he is off a little one way or the other.

The Husky is keeping its growls low and quieter than it did earlier. Quiet enough that the Bigfoot is watching Alex's window and not Joe's window. Allowing Joe to adjust his stance; as needed; as the Bigfoot moves closer to the wall of the house.

Alex is wondering why Joe hasn't shot the creature. She figures he has a good reason but doesn't know what his reasoning is.

She thinks is he waiting to see if any others appear?

Is he worried that if he shoots this one others will appear and attack?

She has these thoughts going through her mind but keeps her trust in him to make the call he sees correct and will provide the best chance for safety.

She is happy to see that the Husky has not jumped out the window to defend Joe.

She thinks it is probably best that the dogs are separated otherwise they may have attacked the Bigfoot. They are bolder when together.

The Bigfoot is getting closer to the wall and the object on the wall.

Joe is keeping the rifle sighted on the Bigfoot as it continues to move closer.

Joe stays to the dark of the room and as close to the wall as possible to still be in position for a shot.

The Bigfoot gets to the object against the wall.

It stares at the closed window and then to Joe's broken window and hesitates at Joe's window. Then looks back to the closed window and stares.

Joe has no doubt it can hear the German Shepard growling because he can hear it over the Husky's growling.

The Bigfoot stands up slowly, rotating its gaze from one window to the other as it stands.

Once it is fully standing Joe estimates the height is similar to the dead one, perhaps a little bigger but not by much. He figures it has to be close, and he figures the weight would be very similar as well.

With the Bigfoot so close Joe has the full effect of the smell and he is trying not to gage on the horrendous stench.

He is able to hold his supper in, so to speak, and does not gage out loud and therefore does not give away his position to the creature.

The Bigfoot reaches out to the object against the wall and takes hold of it.

Alex can hear as the object is twisted and removed from the wall and can even see some debris fall from the inside wall where it almost came through.

Joe heard it being removed as well and watched as the Bigfoot steps away from the wall holding a boulder with both hands.

Joe and Alex, even though in different rooms, they see the same thing and both are amazed at the size of the boulder it is holding.

They would need equipment to even roll the boulder let alone pick it up.

Joe is impressed that the roof is still holding the combined weight of the Bigfoot and the boulder it is now holding.

Now his concern is if he shoots the Bigfoot it will drop the boulder and it will go through the porch roof, even if the Bigfoot escapes the roof it would most likely drop the boulder and make a big hole in the roof.

Joe watches as the Bigfoot steps backward toward the edge of the roof slowly and keeps watching both windows and where the edge of the roof is.

Joe hears the roof creak as it walks backwards with the extra weight in its hands.

The boulder is almost as wide as it is.

It reaches the edge of the roof and another Bigfoot howls.

The one on the roof turns and looks in the direction of the shed where the pickup is parked with the dead one in the bed of the truck.

The Bigfoot on the roof turns its upper body only.

Joe fears this is the re-action before throwing such a large stone. Similar to the way a human would attempt to throw a large, heavy object that they can't use one hand to throw.

Joe takes careful aim and fires at the Bigfoots chest as it is turned away from him for the wind up.

The bullet hits it in the chest just under its left arm below the armpit.

The Bigfoot drops the boulder off the roof and falls off the roof as well screaming in pain.

The sound it makes is deafening and sends chills up and down their spines to hear it.

Alex saw the bullet impact and the Bigfoot drop off the roof after dropping the boulder.

She was grateful to see Joe shot the Bigfoot because she was about to shoot through the window seeing it get ready to throw the stone at the house. At that distance it may have gotten the stone inside, no doubt if it had hit the same spot the stone was removed from.

Joe can hear the Bigfoot on the ground easier than Alex can, she can still hear what sounds similar to a moan in pain.

Joe can also hear, faintly, the way the Bigfoot is struggling to breathe and what he thinks sounds like gurgling as air from lungs mixes with blood from the wound.

Joe is certain it is a killing shot.

Alex and the dog go to Joe.

Joe looks at them and Alex continues to the opposite side of the window across from Joe.

They don't speak and listen and now she can hear the Bigfoot struggling to breathe as well.

They see what they can't believe.

They see the injured Bigfoot running across the yard.

They know it is the injured one because of the blood on its left side.

Half way across the yard it collapses to the ground and lays there.

They then witness three other Bigfoot come out of the darkness and two of them throw rocks of varying sizes at the house while the third one picks up the injured, now believed to be dead, one and carries it into the darkness.

The other two follow after a short time of pelting the house with more stones that they can throw one handed.

Joe whispers to Alex, "I guess we see why no bodies have been found, they carry of the injured and the dead."

Alex nods her agreeance. "But it still doesn't fully explain why no physical remains have been found. Nobody knows if they bury the dead, eat their dead or what they actually do with the dead."

Joe agrees.

They continue watching outside and especially the shed to see if the Bigfoots are still out there in the dark.

They are both thankful that none of the stones the two were throwing hit any windows. If the creatures realize the windows are a weak point in the structure, it could be difficult to defend the house.

It is now midnight and they aren't sure if they are going to be able to sleep tonight or if the Bigfoots will keep them up.

Alex smiles, "We haven't seen midnight since we were dating."

They both laugh.

The laughter is short.

They hear something hitting something out back and they can't see what is making the sound.

Alex asks, "Did you leave the gate to the pasture open?"

Joe looks at her, "No I didn't, and I don't think you were out there today."

Alex, "Yea, I wasn't out there today."

They listen to the sound and it does sound like the gate hitting the metal post it is usually attached to when closed.

They head downstairs and Joe grabs his coat and the spotlight.

Alex grabs his arm, "What if it is a trap and they are wanting one of us to go out there?"

Joe looks at her, "As far as we know they are more animal than human. So for them to have that kind of thought process I'm not sure I would believe it."

Alex, "Yea, but there is more unknown about these things than is known."

Joe, "Good point; but what are we gonna do about the gate. We can't just let the cattle out and spend all day looking for them."

Alex grabs her coat and a flashlight. "I'll go out with you. We can cover each other's back."

Joe agrees and they walk out the door leaving the dogs inside.

They walk slowly.

Joe is using the spotlight to light up everything in the area.

They continue to the gate seeing and hearing nothing other than the gate hitting the post.

They get to the gate and Joe closes it and latches the gate again.

Before leaving the gate he shines the light into the pasture and the cows are still huddled together in a defensive position.

He shines the light around and sees, just at the edge of the lights range, a large figure coming towards them.

He swings the light around the pasture and sees at least three more coming from different areas but all headed straight at them.

He nudges Alex and she turns and sees what is in the light without him pointing them out. He just simply moves the light to show all four that he has seen.

They run for the house.

The closer they get to the house the louder the heavy impacts on the ground get.

It sounds like something large and heavy hitting the ground and they both figure it is the sound of Bigfoots running.

They are closing in on the house but by the sounds of it, the Bigfoots are closing in on them as well.

They don't look behind them and keep running to the house.

As they get to the house, it sounds like more coming in from all sides of them.

They barge into the house and slam the door shut behind

them.

The dogs are quiet and not to be seen.

Joe looks at the clock and it is one o'clock in the morning.

He tells Alex another five to six hours til sunrise roughly.

She looks at him and with a mix of anger and fear, "Do you think they will go away at sunrise?"

Joe, "If they don't we will be able to see them easier and may be able to take out enough to scare the rest away."

Alex agrees with that way of thinking, mainly because she doesn't have a better idea.

Joe watches the areas that are lit and waits for one to enter the light.

But they all seem to stay out of the light and keep to the shadows.

Joe can see shadows move but can't tell if it is a Bigfoot or just tricks his eyes are playing on him thinking shadows are moving.

So he doesn't fire at those movements. He saves his ammo for when he can see the target clearly and know it is not a trick of the eyes.

Alex says she is going to look for the dogs.

Joe agrees and he watches outside as she begins looking for the dogs.

She is praying that nothing has happened to the dogs.

She searches the downstairs first than moves to the second floor.

She finds both dogs sitting and watching the broken window.

The dogs turn and greet her with wagging tails.

While in the room she can hear whistling.

It sounds like there are several tones. She isn't sure if it is several different individuals or a different meaning with the different tones.

She does know there are at least three individuals out there and possibly five perhaps more.

She is only estimating the numbers above three from the sound of at least two more running at them one from each side as they got closer to the house. So she is figuring five but knows of the three they saw crossing the pasture.

She stays back in the dark area of the room out of the light shining in from outside.

She sees movement in the dark just out of the light in the driveway and the motion lights; are going on and off like something is out there triggering the lights, but she can't see what is triggering the motion sensors.

She moves to where she can see the door to the shed where pickup is parked, making sure she stays out of the light.

She notices movement, again just out of the light.

She watches and waits.

She begins to wonder who is the hunted and who is the hunter since Joe and herself are trapped in the house defending themselves from multiple Bigfoots.

She notices a Bigfoot going for the door to the shed.

It is moving slowly and watching the house as it progresses to the shed door.

She raises her rifle and positions her stance for a shot.

The Bigfoot gets to the shed door and is looking at the door.

It reaches out for the lock.

Joe sees the Bigfoot at the shed door and doesn't have a good angle to shoot.

If the bullet passes through the Bigfoot it will enter the shed and who knows what it may hit in there.

Alex is looking at the Bigfoot at the shed door and looks at it through her scope then without and realizes her angle is not good.

She thinks like Joe did, if the bullet passes through the Bigfoots body it will enter the shed and could hit the truck or a piece of equipment.

So now like Joe there is not a good shot to be had on that Bigfoot.

She thinks there has to be a way to get it away from the door. We can't let it get inside there and remove the dead one in the bed of the truck.

She notices movement at the far end of the shed and she watches.

A Bigfoot peeks out around the corner of the far end of the shed and retreats back behind the shed.

The motion light is on behind it and she raises her rifle and takes aim at where she seen it peeking around the corner. She had seen it look around the corner a few times and is hopeful for one more peek.

She doesn't have to wait long. The Bigfoot looks around the corner triggering the motion light with its movement so she can see its head very well in the scope.

She fires and the Bigfoot drops when the bullet hits it in the forehead.

The Bigfoot at the door runs without looking around just runs for the dark.

As the creatures run into the darkness she hears what sounds like screams.

It doesn't sound like the roar or any of the other sounds they were making tonight. The only way she can explain, even to herself, is they screamed.

The one she shot lays dead on the ground.

Joe heard Alex shoot and saw the Bigfoot run from the shed door.

He hopes she didn't take a risky shot that would have risked damaging any equipment inside the shed. He trusts that she would not have taken a shot that would have risked the equipment and figures she had a better angle than he did.

He looks around beyond the front of the shed and sees something laying on the ground at the back corner of the shed before the motion light goes out.

He raises his rifle and finds the object in his scope as the light comes on again and sees a dead Bigfoot on the ground.

He notices the bloody forehead and thinks to himself nice shot.

He lowers his rifle and watches the dead Bigfoot as well as Alex is also watching the dead Bigfoot.

With the motion light on they know something is in that area so they watch.

They see the dead one start to move, but not as if it is alive more like something is trying to pull it from the area that is out of their line of sight.

They watch as the dead Bigfoot is apparently dragged behind the shed and out of sight.

They assume that another Bigfoot is going to carry it away like they did the last one.

But unlike the last one Joe and Alex do not see any other Bigfoot in the area; they are staying to the dark areas outside of the light.

All the motion lights turn off with no motion detected by the sensors.

Joe and Alex are still watching and waiting with rifles ready.

It's now five o'clock and they haven't seen any movement outside in over two hours now.

The last Bigfoot killed was just before three o'clock.

Joe and Alex meet up in the kitchen and have breakfast.

Although they eat differently this morning.

While one of them eats the other is on guard watching outside. They do not let their guard down this morning and neither of them got any sleep all night.

They finish breakfast and still need to do the morning chores.

They need to keep the dairy cow on the same milking schedule so she is where they need her when it is time to milk her and to avoid the risk of the cow getting sick from not milking her.

They know they can't hide in the house forever; they need to come out at some time.

At six o'clock Alex grabs the milk bucket and Joe grabs the spotlight.

They both have their pistols on as they walk to the barn.

Joe shines the light at the shed and checks the doors as they continue walking and the doors look intact with no obvious signs of an attempt to break in.

The dogs are also walking with them. Although not uncommon for the dogs to join them in the barn at milking time this morning the dogs are more alert than usual, looking around and not playing like they normally do.

Joe has the strap over the pistol unsnapped and his hand on it ready to pull it from the holster if he sees a Bigfoot.
While in the barn Alex milks the cow and the dogs stand guard with Joe.

Alex takes care of other barn chores as well while Joe and the dogs stand guard.

She gets the barn cats to come out of hiding. But she is missing one of the cats, and go figure it is one of the better mousers in the barn.

She brushes of the missing cat, it's not the first time one has not showed up for breakfast. The missing cat usually returns within a day or two.

On the way back to the house they hear Bigfoot roars and

Chapter 5
POSESSION OF THE BODY TRANSFERRED

They talk about their options for the day.

They both agree the Bigfoots are watching them and it appears as though they are communicating with others as to what they are doing when outside.

Alex has a thought, "What if they are watching us to see when we open the shed. Then we will find out where the closest one is when it attacks us."

They are still looking out the windows while having this conversation.

Joe shakes his head and then thinks before he responds. "I still am not certain they are that intelligent. However after last night I need to consider that possibility."

Alex, "Remember there isn't much known about these Bigfoots. I am suspecting we have seen a side of them that a lot of Bigfoot Hunters don't want to know about."

Joe agrees. "Most Bigfoot Hunters want to claim these are calm creatures and want to avoid humans. But yet there was one in a tree directly behind you while hunting; and the fact that a bear will not go in the direction of a Bigfoot, not to mention the mountain lion running from the area when a Bigfoot roars. They are apparently more aggressive than most want to believe."

Alex raises her right hand with her pointing finger upright, "Uh my dear, but they will say these creatures are predators and are apparently the top predator in the area they inhabit. You know the shows we have watched they all agree Bigfoot hunts and most likely deer and elk, in the right areas. So why not bear or mountain lions?"

Joe agrees again, "We hunt bear for food, out west they hunt mountain lions and some folk use the meat from them for food so why not Bigfoot. I would suspect they would be less likely to turn down meat of any kind were some humans will not even consider eating a mountain lion because it is a cat or coyote or even wolf, in the right areas, just because it is a dog."

Alex agrees, "I think you are right, the Bigfoot would be less picky when it comes to food. Who's to say they don't or won't eat humans if given a chance? Remember some shows were the people swear the Bigfoot was hunting them? Perhaps they were not thinking that just from fear and they were not exaggerating their experience to make their story more horrifying but they actually were being hunted, most likely as a potential prey item."

Joe nods his head, "You may be onto something there. After last night I'd say anything is possible with those things. I mean look how hard they tried to get inside. Using that large boulder to try and get through the wall. Heaven forbid they figure out the windows are a weak point in the house structure. If that one would have realized that window was broken and came inside before we got upstairs last night could have ended completely different."

Alex nods, "We can verify from last night they can see in the dark. They prefer the dark areas of the yard over the lit areas. Perhaps not just because we can't see them in the dark and giving them a chance to not get shot but because they have an advantage over us in the dark."

Joe again nods as he answers, "I believe you are on the right track babe. What do you think we can do to shift the advantage back to us?"

Alex lowers her head as she thinks about her response. She begins speaking with her head still lowered, "I think we need to start by adding lights to the dark areas around the yard." She raises her head as she continues to speak, "Let's put light where there is no light. Especially close to the house, let's make a gauntlet, so to speak, that they need to run through to reach the house. One that gives us warning of their approach and a clear line of site that we can take them out one at a time as we need too."

Joe smiles, "I knew there was a reason I still love you. That should, at least in theory, transfer the advantage to us. Providing of course we can stay awake all night to protect ourselves."

Alex agrees, "How about one of get a few hours of sleep now and the other gets sleep this afternoon. So we can defend the house all night. That way one of us is up if they come in during the day."

Joe nods his head, "Ok, you go get some rest and I will take the first watch. I will work on removing the boulder from the yard and start repairs to the side of the house."

Bigfoot's Revenge

Alex agrees and she heads to bed.

It is eight o'clock and she sets the alarm for noon. She figures it will allow Joe a few hours of sleep before dark and they find out if they need to defend the house again.

Joe lets the dogs out before he goes to work on anything giving them a chance to go potty.

The dogs, however, just sit on the back porch and do not leave it. Instead they sit there looking around, which is unusual for the dogs because they usually play and run around the yard.

So Joe brings them back inside so he can work and not watch the dogs at the same time.

As he goes out the door he tells the dogs to stay.

Joe has his 44 mag revolver and decides to carry his 25-06 rifle as well. He carries the rifle across his back with the sling he has on the rifle to keep it from interfering with his work, as much as possible.

After he goes out the dogs run and jump in bed with Alex.

Joe goes out to the tractor with the front end loader with a back hoe attachment as well and starts it. While it is warming up he is looking around and sees nothing. The cattle even appear to have relaxed as they are no longer in a defensive group; they have spread out and are grazing.

Once the tractor is warmed up and the hydraulics work like they are supposed to and not sluggish, he goes to the boulder in the yard by the house.

He raises the back hoe bucket and rolls it behind the boulder to roll or slide the boulder farther from the house before he attempts the pick it up with the loader bucket by putting it in the bucket. He is figuring it won't load easily and may slide ahead of the bucket instead of going inside of the bucket.

He manages to get the boulder farther from the house and is able to get to it from a different angle that does not push the boulder towards the house if it doesn't load easily.

He comes in from the downhill side of the boulder to use gravity to assist with the loading of the boulder.

He does manage to get the boulder loaded into the bucket so it stays after he rolls the bucket all the way back towards himself. The boulder seems to have fit in the bucket, enough, to stay in place.

He travels slowly not trusting the boulder since it is not completely seated inside the bucket.

He takes it to the old stone fence bordering the hay field and dumps the boulder on top of the old fence. He then returns the tractor to its parking spot and shuts it down to wait for another job.

He checks his phone and has a missed call and new voicemail from Juanita.

He listens to the voicemail and she says she should be at the farm around noon.

He figures that is perfect. It gives him a chance to work on the house until then.

He gets his measuring tape and goes to the room with the broken window.

He measures the opening so he can find out how big he needs to make the replacement window.

He has his measurements in his notebook and takes some of the window frame pieces that survived so he can make sure the replacement fits correctly.

He goes to another shed, not the wagon/equipment shed where the body is but a smaller storage shed where he has old windows stored.

He finds replacement windows, top and bottom that meet the needed measurements so he takes them with him to the house and goes to the room and installs them.

With that job done he looks at his watch and it is ten o'clock, actually a few minutes after but not a full five minutes so he rounds the time backwards.

The dogs are in the room and seem to give their approval of the replacement window.

He goes to the next room and looks at the damage to the interior wall. He pulls the drywall from the wall to see it any of the wall studs are damaged.

He finds two that are in need of repair. They are too damaged to trust without repairing. They are actually broken completely through.

He opens the wall more to see the studs next to the broken ones and sees they are still good. The boulder apparently hit between the two broken studs and was big enough to break both of them. It appears the boulder only hit that one area of the house whether it was thrown once or more he doesn't know for sure. If it was only one throw then the Bigfoot that threw it is much stronger then he would have ever imagined.

He removes the drywall that is connected to the two studs and then removes the insulation between the studs so he can get his measurements. He then goes to the storage shed and gets two, two by fours to cut to length to put one piece of two by four in next to the broken studs to repair the broken studs by adding these to those. So the wall will still have the structural strength that it needs. He is not removing the broken studs just adding these new studs to the wall as replacements.

He puts the insulation back in between the studs but he doesn't have any drywall to replace what was removed from the wall. But he does take the measurements of the size of the hole he needs to repair so he knows how many sheets of drywall he will need to buy.

He opens the window and climbs out onto the roof to start removing the broken siding off the house.

He hears coyotes and they sound close.

He looks around and sees three coyotes sniffing around the shed where the dead Bigfoot is being kept.

He remembers that some people think Bigfoot works with coyotes either as pets or as hunting partners nobody has figured it out except that they do run together at times.

Joe looks around and doesn't see any sign of any Bigfoot for as far as he can see.

He removes the rifle from his back and before he raises it he remembers Alex is sleeping and doesn't want to wake her up with the sound of the rifle going off. She may think the Bigfoots are attacking.

Instead he sits on the porch roof and watches the coyotes as they continue sniffing around and then leave heading towards the trees where Alex's tree stand is located.

The cattle are not bothered by the coyotes running through the pasture and just go about grazing.

Joe looks at his watch and it is now 11:45; so he gets measurements for a quick patch to the hole, his plan is to just cut a piece of plywood to cover the hole.

As it turns out he will need a full sheet of plywood, 8 feet by 4 feet, to cover the hole in the wall.

He goes back inside through the window and then downstairs and out to the storage shed for a sheet of plywood.

He gets the plywood out and over to the house then gets his extension ladder off the side of the wagon/equipment shed, the shed with the pickup and dead Bigfoot inside, and takes it the house and sets it up to the porch roof. He retrieves a battery powered drill and screws as well before going up the ladder.

Before heading up the ladder Alex appears on the porch and before she says anything he sees a small refrigerated truck turn into the driveway.

They stand there and wait to see if it is whom they think it is.

The truck pulls up and a lady gets out of the passenger side and comes around to them.

She reaches out her hand and introduces herself and Juanita.

Joe and Alex take turns shaking her hand.

Juanita apologizes for interrupting the repairs it looks like he is working on as she points to the ladder.

Joe smiles, "I only have the repairs to do because a Bigfoot through a boulder into the side of our house." He points to the hole in the wall.

Juanita looks at the hole and is surprised, "Bigfoot did that? How?"

Joe looks at her, "With that boulder over there on the fence row." He points to the stone.

Juanita and her driver look over to the stone.

Juanita, "You mean, Bigfoot throw that big stone and make the hole in wall?"

Joe, "Yes, we also witnessed a Bigfoot lifting the stone to throw it at the house again. I stopped it from throwing the stone."

Juanita's driver asks, "How, how did you stop it from throwing the stone again?"

Joe looks at him.

Juanita speaks up before Joe answers, "I sorry, this Steve my driver."

Joe nods to Juanita in acknowledgement then looks at Steve, "Well Steve, I shot that Bigfoot before it could throw it. The Bigfoot pulled the stone from the wall, yes they threw it hard enough it was stuck in the wall, then it walked backwards, watching where it was at in relation to the end of the roof and when it turned its upper body and not its lower body I shot it in the chest."

Steve, "Did you kill it?"

Joe, "Yes, it dropped the stone, then it fell off the roof and got up and ran half way across the yard before collapsing to the ground."

Juanita, "You sure it dead? You have it also?"

Joe, "No we don't have any more than the one you came to pick up. We are sure it is dead because another Bigfoot carried it away."

Juanita, "Oh, Ok can we load the one you have for me then I look at big stone and measure. Maybe get estimate, with computer help, how strong it may be."

Joe, "No problem, but first you need to measure the rock. The others are watching and waiting for us to open this door." He points to the shed door. "They know the dead one is in there and we had to kill two of them last night defending ourselves."

Juanita is again surprised, "You mean you kill two more? But you say you have one body?"

Joe, "Yes the others carried off the two we shot here at the house defending ourselves."

Steve, "You know these creatures are docile right?"

Alex starts laughing out loud, "Docile, docile," she points in the direction of her tree stand. "You go over there and stand, I'd say you wouldn't need to wait long today, and if you make it back here then you tell us if you still believe they are docile creatures. We have seen the aggression in them, perhaps it was from me accidently killing one of them but either way we killed two more last night. We are sleeping in shifts today so one of us is on guard at all times. Docile, when one of the creatures throws a large stone at your house then you tell me if you still believe they are docile."

Joe puts his hand on Alex's shoulder, "Babe go get your rifle and pistol on so we can supply cover for loading the dead one when it is time, and we can offer protection while they measure the stone."

Alex agrees and goes inside.

Juanita, "Is that why you have guns with you now?"

Joe, "Yes."

Joe, "I had to use my tractor with the back hoe and loader to remove the stone from beside the house. Actually there is another stone inside that they threw through an upstairs window last night that is going to take Alex and myself together to remove it because of the size of it."

Chapter 5

Juanita looks at Steve then back to Joe, "Can we have that stone?"

Alex comes out at the end of the question.

Joe looks at her, "Of course, we would just take it to the fence row to be with the other stones."

Alex looks at him, "Which stone do they want?"

Joe, "The one that is still upstairs."

Alex, "Oh, I suppose we can load that one."

Joe goes to the storage shed and gets his One hundred foot tape to measure the big stone.

Joe hands the tape to Juanita, "Alex and I will need our hands free to protect us if the Bigfoots come out."

Juanita nods and takes the tape.

They all walk over to the stone.

Joe and Alex have their heads on a swivel they are scanning the area so much.

Before they reach the stone Joe tells them to stop and let him check that it is safe beyond the stone. That nothing is hiding behind the stone, he mentions the bear and mountain lion in the area to worry about not just the Bigfoots.

Joe goes ahead and Alex stays behind to cover if something comes in from behind.

Joe looks around the stone and even beyond as far as he can see and gives the all clear so the group moves up to the stone.

Joe and Alex stand on the stone fence row facing opposite directions while Juanita and Steve take the measurements of the stone.

As they get started on measuring the stone a Bigfoot roars. Not real close but close enough they can still feel it in their bodies.

Joe and Alex put the rifle stocks to their shoulder with the barrel still pointing down to the ground.

Juanita and Steve are excited.

Juanita, "Was that a Bigfoot?"

Joe, "Yes."

Alex, "And it sounded like it is in the area of your tree stand."

Joe, "Yes, can you see the tree stand?"

Juanita and Steve look at Joe.

Alex, "Not specifically no."

Joe, "Can you at least find the tree the stand is in?"

Alex, "Trade me positions; you know your tree better than I

do. You look for it."

They swap positons.

Alex gives him a couple minutes while Juanita and Steve go back to measuring.

Alex, "Do you see your stand?"

Joe, "I see the tree yes. I can't make out the stand but if nothing destroyed it than it should be just on the crest of the hill just barely visible."

Juanita and Steve are not in a hurry by any stretch of the imagination. They are taking their measurements slowly, most likely for accuracy when it comes time to do the computer side of the experiment trying to estimate the weight of the stone.

Joe sees movement in his tree stand.

He watches as it appears to stand upright. He sees it move as they hear another roar from the area of his stand.

This roar sounds different from the first one. It sounded more aggressive.

Joe tells them to hurry up with the measuring because we are being watched.

Alex doesn't look back to him but keeps here focus in her direction. "What do you see Hun?"

Juanita looks in the direction Joe is looking, "Do you see one?"

Joe points, "Do you see that large tree?"

Juanita, "Yes."

Joe keeps his focus on the object in the tree. "You see something in the tree that isn't the tree?"

Steve is now looking as well.

Juanita is looking and she sees movement, "Oh my goodness, is that Bigfoot in the tree?"

Joe, "Yes, are you done measuring?"

Juanita, "No, need more measurement."

Joe, "Please finish quickly. It just jumped out of the tree stand."

Steve's fear is starting to show in his voice, "Are we safe to finish?"

Joe, "Finish quickly; Alex and I will hold them off if we need too. But they are smart and most likely will not attack knowing we are standing here."

Alex, "We have already killed three of them so they may be

less likely to attack."

Joe sees a Bigfoot appear on the top of the hill.

Joe with urgency in his voice, "We have one above us, Babe keep alert all around."

Alex, "I am, you stay alert as well, don't focus only on the one. The one we don't see will be the one that gets us."

Joe agrees verbally and keeps looking around but keeps attention on the one on the hill.

Juanita, "We done, we can go now."

Juanita looks up the hill and sees the one standing upright. She is amazed how big it is at two hundred plus yards away.

Joe tells Alex to take the lead back to the house.

Alex, "Honey I should take the rear since I had sleep and you haven't yet. That way if it comes at us I will be quicker on the draw than you."

Joe doesn't look at her, "Babe just go, I got the rear you lead."

Alex takes the lead and Juanita and Steve keep looking back as they run for the house.

Joe is looking back as well. The Bigfoot is standing there watching them run.

The Bigfoot on the hill roars, loader than the previous roars. After the roar Joe yells to stop.

They group stops.

Alex doesn't turn around, "Why did you tell us to stop?"

Joe, "I watched the Bigfoot roar, it was louder yes. But it also was watching towards the house. I think we've been set up. The buggers are smarter than I gave them credit for."

Alex, "Wait you think there are more at the house now?"

Joe, "If not at the house than nearby."

Joe raises his rifle and takes aim at the one on the hill.

That Bigfoot apparently sees Joe raise the rifle and it drops to the ground and disappears quickly away from view on the top of the hill.

Joe couldn't tell if it ran on all fours or not. He just knows it is gone before he could even get it in the scope.

Joe motions to Alex to come to him, he goes towards her as well.

Once together; Joe speaks in a voice just loud enough to be heard. "Babe, you take Juanita and Steve and go slowly around the front of the shed, I will go around the back of the shed. If they are trying to ambush us they may not have figured on us splitting up the group."

Alex agrees and she informs Juanita and Steve then they move slowly around the front as Joe moves slowly around the back of the shed.

The Bigfoot on the hill behind them roars.

Joe turns around and raises his rifle again the Bigfoot drops out of site.

Joe turns back around to continue moving around the shed.

Alex stops her group as she looks under the truck to be sure there isn't anything on the other side of it.

She motions with her hand to continue after she is sure there is nothing to be concerned about behind the truck.

They all see each other on the other side of the shed.

Joe walks over to Alex, Juanita and Steve.

Steve, "What do you think the Bigfoot was saying when it roared?"

Joe, "I don't know, perhaps it was telling the others what we were doing and to stay out of sight."

Alex, "I saw you raise your rifle at the one on the hill a couple times, why didn't you shoot?"

Joe, "I disappeared before I could get the rifle completely in position and find it in the scope. It looked like it just dropped out of sight."

Joe looks at Steve, "I need you to turn your truck around so we can load this thing quickly and you can leave without having to turn around."

Steve nods and gets in the truck and works on turning it around.

Steve gets turned around and is back in front of the shed.

Joe asks if they still want the stone inside the house to take with them.

Juanita says yes they definitely want that stone.

Joe tells them to wait while he and Alex get the stone.

Joe and Alex go inside and return with the stone.

They used an old king size flat sheet and folded in quarter and cradled the stone in the sheet so they could team carry the stone to the truck. They were going to cut the old sheet up for rags so this use is not a loss of a good sheet.

Once they come out Steve opens the back of the truck and Joe and Alex lift the stone into the truck for them. Then Joe goes to the shed and unlocks the door and hands Steve the keys to the pickup to pull it out and park it next to the refrigerated box truck they brought.

Juanita is curious, "Why you not move you own truck?"

Joe is scanning one direction as Alex is scanning the other direction.

Joe, "So we are not left one rifle short on defense."

Juanita, "You think they will attack?"

Joe nods while answering, "Yes I do believe they will. I am sure they knew this one was in here and they were trying to get to it last night."

Juanita raises her head as if to agree and say oh at the same time.

Steve gets the pickup into position and puts it in park, turns it off and gets out.

Juanita started unwrapping the tarp around the Bigfoot before Steve got out of the truck.

Juanita has the Bigfoot completely unwrapped by the time Steve gets to the back of the truck.

They both get the full effect of the odor from the Bigfoot.

Juanita, "I thought you said this was shot yesterday?"

Alex doesn't look away from her surveillance direction, "It was; I shot it in the afternoon."

Juanita, "Smell like it been dead weeks already."

Joe catches a whiff of the odor, "No that is their odor. You are welcome to take that tarp it is wrapped in with you."

Juanita is looking at the face of the Bigfoot, "It does look very human. Is amazing how much look human."

Joe, "Yes it does look more human than expected."

Juanita and Steve wrap the tarp around the Bigfoot again and begin moving it to the refrigerated box for transport to New Jersey.

They hear a Bigfoot roar. It is loud and not real close but close enough that Alex and Joe put rifle to shoulder with barrel pointing down for a quick raise of the rife.

More Bigfoot roars from all around them.

Joe tells Juanita and Steve to get it loaded quickly.

The Bigfoot roars are loud and there are multiple creatures and the roars are running together and even at the same time.

The roars are sounding more aggressive the longer they keep going.

There are now howls and screams mixed in with the roars.

Juanita and Steve are struggling to move the dead Bigfoot but do manage to work together to get it into the box truck.

Once the body is loaded they close the doors.

Steve checks the temperature of the refrigerator unit and it is acceptable temp considering the colder outside temperature.

Joe can see movement on the hill top but can't see what exactly is moving.

Alex sees movement in the tree line below the pasture but can't see exactly what is moving.

They both suspect the Bigfoots are the movement but will not shoot unless they are sure of the target and if the Bigfoots decide to charge.

Steve gets in the truck and starts it.

Juanita starts the thank Joe and Alex.

Joe interrupts her, "Not to be disrespectful, but you need to go before they decide to stop being nice."

Juanita agrees and gets in the truck and they leave.

Joe and Alex stand watching as the truck leave the driveway then go inside the house.

They are not inside long when Joes phone rings.

He answers it seeing it is Juanita, "Hello."

Juanita the fear is obvious in her voice, "We are stopped by Bigfoot, many of them all around truck."

Joe, "Ok we will try to get them out of your way."

Joe doesn't hang up but Juanita does.

Alex, "What is going on?"

Joe tells her and then they go upstairs to their room that has windows facing the road in the direction that Steve and Juanita went.

They have their rifles in hand.

When they get to the room and the windows they carefully check outside each window they will use to be sure there is no Bigfoot outside waiting for them to open a window.

They are satisfied there are no Bigfoots on the porch roof.

Joe and Alex open separate windows slowly trying to avoid being detected by any of the Bigfoot.

They get the windows open enough for them to kneel down

and use the window sill as a rifle prop and a more accurate shot by removing body movement that would affect the rifles aim.

Joe asks Alex which one she has a better shot at, in the front of the truck.

Alex tells him, "The one on the right side of the truck."

Joe, "Ok; I will take the one on the left side and hopefully the one in the middle will run away; as well as the rest will hopefully run away."

Joe and Alex both realize that puts them shooting in an X pattern. But they don't mention it and line up on the Bigfoot that they decided on to help Juanita and Steve.

Alex asks, "How far do you think that is, roughly."

Joe looks at the distance, "I'd guestimate about five hundred yards give or take a few yards. Just remember to aim a little high."

Joe adds, "Let's shoot on three."

Alex agrees believing that will confuse the Bigfoots by only hearing one shot and two of them get hit and hopefully increases the chance to help Juanita and Steve.

Joe begins the count.

As he counts the Bigfoots are closing in on the box truck from all sides.

Joe and Alex can hear the Bigfoots communicating or what they believe is communication.

It does sound like a bunch of whistles, growls, grunts and perhaps low volume roars but at the distance they are not certain it is the Bigfoots they hear.

Joe reaches three and they both shoot with only a very small fraction of second between shots. It still sounded like one shot so they achieved that goal at least.

The two Bigfoots that were targeted both hit the ground and roll away from the road.

The other remaining Bigfoots run from the road and didn't look around before running.

Joe and Alex pull the rifles inside and stay low to watch as Steve drives away and the two Bigfoots that were shot get up and go into the woods.

Alex, "Do you think we should finish them off while we can still see them?"

Joe shakes his head, "No babe, they will die. Remember the one on the roof, it ran and then collapsed later. Just let them go and let's stay out of sight for now."

Alex agrees and they stay low at the windows and watch.

The box truck with Steve and Juanita disappear from their line of sight.

They hear the unmistakable sound of a Bigfoot roaring, just as loud as they have heard before.

They know, or at least believe, the creatures are several hundred yards away and yet that sounded a lot closer.

Joe and Alex stay low just watching.

They see several Bigfoots run in the direction the box truck went.

Alex is curious, "Do you think they are chasing the truck?"

Joe, "If I had to guess I would say it looks like they are."

Alex, "Wow they must really want that one back."

Joe agrees.

It appears that the Bigfoots are not watching the house so they stand up and close the windows.

Joe thinks he sees something and asks Alex if she sees it and even though she also sees it neither can say for sure it is a Bigfoot watching them.

Chapter 6
PREPARING FOR THE NIGHT

The thing they see doesn't move and appears to be a stump of a tree long removed by the county.

It's one thirty now so Joe goes to bed while Alex stays up and keeps watch the rest of the day.

Joe sets the alarm for five pm and goes to sleep.

Alex goes downstairs and the dogs follow.

The dogs seem to prefer sharing the bed with Alex over Joe.

Alex goes outside and the dogs follow her.

She goes to the storage shed and the dogs play.

She gathers up some solar powered motion lights they had bought and never put up.

She goes around the side of the house that they had decided would get the lights and she starts deciding where to put the lights.

They don't have any solar powered lights up and don't know how well they will work.

She proceeds with placing the lights at the base of trees and poles to put them up.

As she goes for the ladder she notices the dogs have stopped playing and are staying close to her.

She watches the dogs as she continues to work wanting to see what they are so protective about now.

She is figuring there is at least one Bigfoot in the area but she can't see it and she knows that doesn't mean the dogs don't hear or smell it even if they can't see it.

She puts the ladder up at the first pole and goes up with everything she needs to mount the light to the pole.

She does have her 30-06 rifle on her back and her 357 pistol on her side just in case she may need one or the other.

She gets to the position where she wants to mount the light and hears a Bigfoot roar.

It sounds like it is below her across the pasture.

Still she can't see it.

Both dogs are sitting next to the ladder on the ground starring in the direction of the roar.

She continues putting the light up and looks around every so often.

She gets the first light mounted and moves to the next location.

The dogs are staying close enough that she almost trips over them. She even hits them with the ladder as she is moving it and putting it in position; she didn't hurt either dog but got their attention.

She continues mounting the lights as the dogs continue guarding her.

She gets to the last light and still has not seen a Bigfoot.

She has heard more sounds she believes is a Bigfoot but has not seen one.

The dogs are moving their stare from one area to another. Especially when she is mounting the light closest to the road.

While in the tree, after mounting the light but before descending the ladder she looks across the road. To the area where she and Joe thought they saw an old stump. The stump isn't there anymore.

She scans further up and down the road thinking she is looking in the wrong place but she can't find the stump.

Now she is concerned because that means a Bigfoot was watching them.

She looks at the dogs and they are still scanning from one area to another, not focusing on one area to long.

She climbs down and begins putting everything away.

This project took her longer than she anticipated and Joe will soon be getting up.

She gets everything put away and the trash in the can, the burnable items are separated to be burnt later.

She and the dogs go inside as a Bigfoot roars again.

This time it sounds like it is above her where the one watched them load the dead one into the box truck.

She grabs her rifle and turns around but sees nothing.

The dogs are waiting at the door for her.

She gets the impression the dogs don't want anything to do with the Bigfoots.

She goes inside and puts the rifle in a corner and starts supper.

Joe gets up and comes down stairs.

Alex tells him about the lights taking longer than expected but they are up and about the stump not being there anymore. She asks him to go look for it just to be sure she didn't miss it.

Joe goes to a window and looks around, up and down the road and doesn't see the stump either but he does notice the placement of the light.

He goes back to her and says he can't find the stump either and compliments her on her light placement.

She smiles.

She turns the stovetop off and they go out to do the evening milking of the cow.

Joe grabs his rifle, puts his revolver on his side and grabs the rechargeable spotlight.

Alex has her pistol still on her side.

The dogs follow.

The dogs seem to be their playful selves on the way to the barn this evening. Until a Bigfoot roars, then the dogs, Joe and Alex are all looking in the direction the sound came from.

Joe shoulders his rifle keeping the barrel pointing down; Alex grabs the handle on her pistol but keeps it in the holster. The dogs are alert and staying close.

Joe and Alex neither one sees the Bigfoot so they continue into the barn to do the evening chores.

Again Alex milks the cow and feeds the barn animals while Joe keeps watch.

The dogs decide to lay down and take a nap.

The barn cat that was missing in the morning is still missing.

Joe notices a scent in the air that is not barn scent. It has a different odor and doesn't match the normal barn smell, it is mixed with the barn odor which makes it more difficult to notice or determine what exactly he is \smelling.

Joe takes notice to which way the breeze is coming from and watches that direction.

There is a window they keep open for ventilation.

Joe watches that window until Alex is finished. He sees nothing and isn't sure if there is anything there to be concerned about, he thinks it was the odor of a Bigfoot but without visual evidence he brushes it off.

With the barn chores done they head back to the house.

The dogs are not playing but are again on alert which puts

Joe and Alex on alert as well with darkness approaching.

They hear sounds that they believe are the Bigfoots communicating.

Some of the sounds they never considered before but now they are cautious and remain alert.

Some sounds are what the Bigfoot hunters refer as tree knocks and before all this happened Joe and Alex both believed those sounds were just dead limbs falling in the woods that they would be able to hear. But now after all this has been going on they believe it to be the Bigfoots in the area especially considering the amount of sounds they hear when outside now. Neither one believes there is that many tree limbs or entire trees falling while they are outside. Granted they don't know how much is going on while they are inside. But the activity; with the sounds do increase closer to dark.

Chapter 7
A MOSTLY QUIET NIGHT

They get back inside the house and Alex continues making supper while Joe keeps watch outside.

The dogs find a spot to lay down and take a nap.

As darkness arrives he can see less outside.

In the last of the light before total darkness Joe thinks he sees movement but isn't sure and continues to watch.

Alex has supper ready and puts everything on the table.

They sit down to eat.

Alex is a little confused, "Shouldn't one of us keep watch tonight while we eat?"

Joe shrugs his shoulders, "Perhaps, but I haven't seen anything out there tonight. I thought I seen some movement but couldn't be sure it wasn't my eyes playing tricks on me in the low light. I never seen the motion light come on anyway so I figure it was just me and not actual movement. Besides; the dogs will let us know if they hear anything tonight. Hopefully with the dead one gone things will go back to normal and we can all share the farm again."

Alex tilts her head to one side, "Suppose you have a point. But we killed how many, three that we are sure of and possibly two more so Juanita and Steve could leave. Do you really think they will leave us alone?"

Joe adds a head tilt to his shoulder shrug, "I am hoping they will leave us alone and give us the opportunity to do the same to leave them alone."

Alex shakes her head, "I hope you are right. Hate to think we will have to fight them every night for God knows how long. Until they give up and leave the farm or loose too many of their group."

Joe nods since he just took a bite of food.

They finish supper and then wash the dishes like a normal night.

After the dishes are washed, dried and put away Alex asks, "Are we going to stand guard tonight at all?"

Joe thinks and tilts his head as he speaks, "Well, how about we give them a chance to leave us alone. In other words, let's not provoke them tonight by standing at the windows watching for them and let's not kill any tonight unless we absolutely have too."

Alex, "What do you mean absolutely have too?"

Joe, "Well if one were to make its way inside for instance."

Alex looks at him, "You have lost your blooming mind. You've seen how fast they can move."

Joe nods his head, "Yeah I did see that, but they appear to be fairly intelligent creatures. Perhaps they will understand if they don't attack us we won't kill any of them."

Alex shakes her head again, "I still say you lost your blooming mind. But I am keeping the pistol with me just in case."

Joe agrees, "I will also keep my pistol just in case."

They settle into their normal routine and sit down to watch tv for a while.

They do keep looking out the windows every time one of them gets up and while watching tv they look at the windows in the living room to see if anything is peeking in at them.

Everything is quiet tonight.

They don't see anything outside when they look.

None of the motion lights near the house are coming on.

So Alex is thinking that Joe may have a point with his way of thinking, no matter how stupid she thinks the thought is.

They turn the lights off in the house at the usual time that they go to bed.

But they do not go to bed, they just go through the normal routine making it seem like they are.

Turning on the lights upstairs in the bathroom and bedroom and turn the lights off as usual.

Joe is hopeful that the Bigfoots will not bother them but if they stay up and make the Bigfoots think they went to bed then they will find out for sure.

All is quiet, Joe and Alex are watching out the windows and no motion lights have been triggered tonight.

Alex is really starting to think that Joe's idiotic idea may prove to be right. But of course she keeps that thought to herself.

It is now midnight and nothing has happened, not even a motion light has been triggered.

They hear nothing and the dogs have given no indication to anything being outside.

Chapter 7

Joe and Alex fall asleep, the dogs were already asleep.

About one thirty they wake up to the sound of metal being hit.

They look out the windows and see the pickup is gone.

Joe grabs the spotlight and shines it around and sees the pickup in the hay field.

It is barely recognizable as a vehicle let alone a pickup truck.

He goes for the door and Alex stands in his way.

Alex, "You ain't going out there in the dark."

Joe looks at her with the anger he has for the Bigfoot at that moment.

She sees the anger in his eyes and doesn't back down. She has faith that he will not hurt her.

Joe; with the anger showing in his voice. "They are destroying the pickup. We need that vehicle and don't have the money to replace it."

Alex isn't making any attempt to hide her anger, she lets it be known.

Alex stays in front of the door, "Did we see the same vehicle? It looked pretty well destroyed already, there is no way we can still use it. We still don't know if the Bigfoots will kill us or not if we go out there. I ain't about to just let you go out there and find out if they will make you look like the truck or if they will sit down and talk this out like the civilized beings they ain't."

Joe looks at her, "I know you're right but they killed the truck."

Alex calms down a little, "I know that, I could see that as well. But if you rush out there and disregard all safety precautions. And you shoot at the first thing that moves and don't think it through then what? Do you think they won't attack from behind, out of the dark? Do you honestly believe that if you fire a single shot, whether you hit one or not that they won't retaliate tonight? For God's sake look what they did to the truck. Remember the size of that rock we saw one pull out of the wall and get ready to throw at the house again. Remember the size of the rock we carried out together for Juanita. Do you really think after everything we have been through the last thirty six or so hours that those creatures mean no harm?"

Joe lowers his head, "I understand all that, and I do remember the size of those rocks." Joe raises his head and looks her in the eye, "But if we do nothing will they stop? Or will they begin to think they have the power over us and can do whatever they want without recourse?"

Alex shakes her head, "I don't know. Nobody does, we are the first that have had an encounter to this degree and lived to tell about it, so far. At least to my knowledge, I know I haven't heard of anything like this. Ok the Bigfoot hunters that are out there trying to kill one they go to some aggressive cases but not on this scale."

Joe smiles, "Maybe we can contact them and get them to help."

Alex smiles and shakes her head, "Where are they again? Somewhere in the south if I remember, how long would it take them to get here? Do you think we can survive the days it would take for them to get here or would we already be dead at the hands of the Bigfoot?"

Joe, "We don't know for sure the Bigfoots will kill us babe."

Alex shakes her head again, "Do you really think those things out there won't kill us if given a chance. They are still stalking us at night. They are even watching us during the day, you heard the calls they make every time we go outside."

Joe nods his head.

They hear heavy footsteps on the porch behind Alex.

She and Joe move away from the door.

Joe has his rifle in hand and Alex has her pistol in her hand as they face the door.

He motions to Alex to watch the door as he moves around to see out the window.

He sees a motion light on out at the barn and it lights a large figure on the porch. He figures it must be a Bigfoot but can't see for sure that it is.

Joe points to the light switch and Alex reaches out and turns on the porch light.

When the light turns on Joe sees it is a Bigfoot and it sees him in the light shining in through the window and it howls and runs off in a direction Alex put lights up and it triggers on of the motion sensors for the light. It howls again and keeps running.

They decide to leave the porch light on.

Alex looks at Joe and doesn't hold back. "See, there was one close. It would have had you before you got too far off the porch."

Joe, "I see that. But we don't know for sure they will kill us."

Alex shakes her head, "When will you wake the snot up? That thing was not up her to kiss us and invite us to dinner unless we would be the dinner."

Joe, "We don't know, it could have been curious."

Alex, "Yeah, curious about how to work the door. Curious about if we were actually asleep or not. Curious about how to get in."

Joe, "Or curious if we would actually shoot it or not."

Alex nods, "But we don't know. It's not like we can talk to them and say we are sorry about the dead, we were only defending ourselves. The first death was an accident and we didn't mean for the death to happen. It's not like we can have a conversation and explain our side and understand their side. To be able to tell them if they leave us in peace we will in turn leave them in peace, we can share the farm and the game."

They sit down and watch outside and the motion activated lights don't come on again the rest of the night.

They don't hear anything either, on the porch or sounds they would count as coming from a Bigfoot.

They nod in and out of sleep the rest of the night.

After the sun starts to rise and they can see; they head out to the barn to do the morning milking and feedings.

They go in the barn and the milk cow isn't in her stall.

They search the barn thinking maybe she is taking her time this morning and they do not find her in the barn at all.

They look in the pasture and don't see her there either.

Joe looks around on the ground and in the soft manure in the barnyard he sees Bigfoot tracks.

He points them out to Alex.

They can see where a Bigfoot went into the barn and the tracks coming out of the barn sank into the manure much deeper like it gained a lot of weight before leaving.

They can see the tracks are heading in the direction of Alex's tree stand.

Alex looks at Joe, "We have to go after her. We can't let them kill her."

Joe looks at her, "Babe it was able to carry a full grown dairy cow over a thousand pounds of cow. It left no drag marks, which means it carried her away. You were the one against going after them last night now you want to go after them."

Alex looks in the direction the footprints are leading. "Yeah I want to go after them now. They took Carmen. She was; is the best milk cow we ever had."

Joe, "Ok, let's get loaded up and head out looking for Carmen."

They go back to the house and Alex gets her rifle and they make sure they have extra ammo for rifles and pistols.

They make sure the dogs stay inside the house when they leave.

Joe looks over at the pickup.

Alex smacks his shoulder, "Carmen first."

Chapter 8
THEIR STORY IS OUT

Alex, "Why do you think it carried Carmen and didn't just lead her out? Because if she was lead out that would not leave drag marks either."

Joe, "Your right it wouldn't, but you saw the tracks. The Bigfoot was approximately twice the weight when it came out as to when it went in. Unless you think it sat in the barn and ate her before leaving."

Alex looks at him, "I don't want to think about that at this time."

Joe, "You know we were going to eat her when she wouldn't produce milk anymore. Once she quit having calves."

Alex, "I know, that is the way we have done it for a long time. But this is different; we don't know how they kill if it is quick or if their prey suffers."

They cross the pasture following the path the Bigfoot left.

It was heavy enough the grass is laid down in the direction of travel.

They get to the fence and Joe looks at the fence then to Alex.

Joe, "The fence is still intact do you still want to think she was led away?"

Alex looks at him, "Ok, she must have been carried. But to think it could cross the fence while carrying her." She shakes her head in disbelieve.

Joe and Alex cross the fence and pick up the trail again on the other side of the road.

It's a little harder to see the trail but the leaves are moved like the Bigfoot was partly dragging its feet.

Joe thinks to himself that maybe the Bigfoot is getting tired of carrying the cow.

Alex looks toward her tree stand and the trail appears to be heading in that direction.

They continue following the trail between the corn and the trees.

Alex keeps looking toward her stand, looking in the trees to see if they are being watched.

She doesn't see anything in the trees even as they get closer, including her tree stand.

She doesn't say anything, doubting herself as to whether she is looking in the right tree.

Unknown to Alex, Joe is also looking for her tree stand and can't see it.

Joe sees that the trail appears to be heading to her stand. Not on the same path she usually took to the stand but still in that direction.

They continue following the trail slowly. Watching as far ahead as they can see; trying to avoid surprising the bear, mountain lion or worse a Bigfoot.

They follow the trail as it goes into the woods.

They get close enough to see where Alex's tree stand is supposed to be, but don't see it in the trees.

They continue following the trail and her tree stand comes into view.

It is laying on the ground and is completely destroyed.

It is now nothing but a pile of twisted and a crushed pile of scrap metal, not even recognizable as a tree stand anymore.

The metal tree stand was painted green but they notice red on the metal as well.

Alex looks at it and asks, "Is that blood?"

Joe leans in and takes a closer look, wanting to be sure someone didn't use red spray paint on it after destroying the stand in an attempt to make it seem like it wasn't done by humans.

Joe stands back up and points to one area, "It looks like blood, and that looks like a large hand print."

Alex looks at the print Joe is pointing out, then she points out the nylon straps are broken not cut like they have had human vandals do before.

Joe is looking around and thinking while he speaks, "If this is a Bigfoot hand print, made with its own blood." He looks over the twisted metal again. "But I am not seeing where it cut itself; there is no obvious evidence on any of the sharp edges that it cut itself."

Alex is walking around the area and looking while Joe is looking at the destroyed tree stand.

Alex speaks up, "I know why there is blood on the metal. It isn't Bigfoot blood it's Carmen's blood." She begins to tear up while speaking and is fighting the emotion to cry as she speaks.

Joe stands and turns to Alex then walks to her.

Now they are both looking at the scattered skeletal remains with enough bloody hide left to be sure it is Carmen's remains.

Joe walks over to the remains that are still wet, he isn't guessing if the moisture is blood or saliva from what was feeding on the remains.

Alex keeps watch as best as she can while trying to control her emotions. She usually got emotional when the have butchered milk cows the entire time they have been married. She has a tendency to get emotionally attached to the cow and consider it as a barn pet but still keeping in mind the reasoning for the animal on the farm.

Joe is better at controlling his emotions and even though he is upset and emotionally distraught over the death of their milk cow. He wants to understand more about what killed her and consumed her remains.

Joe is looking at the bones; he picks them up one at a time to see if he can find teeth marks in the bone and if so try to determine if the marks were made from a canine, like coyote.

As he examines the bones the teeth marks he finds do not resemble canine, nor would he consider the marks to have been made by a mountain lion or even a bear.

To his, untrained eye, the marks look like they were made by something without the sharp teeth associated with the predators like coyotes, mountain lions and even bears. His none expert opinion is that the teeth marks left on the bones resemble human teeth scratching the bone, granted deeper scratches than a human would leave but similar to what human teeth would leave behind.

Joe picks up one of the leg bones with more obvious teeth marks on it to take with them. He hopes to get Juanita to examine the marks and get her expert opinion about the marks.

As they get ready to head back to the house they hear something in the woods but they don't see anything.

They hear sounds in the woods like limbs breaking and objects hitting the ground.

They have rocks landing on the ground near them and even see some of the larger rocks as they are in the air coming towards them. Some of the smaller rocks they see after they land and are still rolling, tumbling for the more oddly shaped rocks.

Bigfoot's Revenge

Joe tells Alex, "Let's get outta here before they hit us with one of those rocks."

Alex agrees and they head for the house. Not a full run but a fast walk and taking turns looking back as they continue to the house.

Before getting to the road they hear Bigfoot vocalizations. Not just roars but whistles and what they believe to be grunts, by the sound, even screams.

At the lab Juanita was met with some unexpected greeters when she arrived for work; this morning.
The greeters were journalists, local, national and even international.

Many of the journalists were screaming questions about the Bigfoot inside. Wanting to know where it came from, is it real, how long have they had it in their possession, how much do they know about the creature? And many other questions were just being thrown at her with no order and the journalists all speaking at the same time demanding answers. These few listed are the questions she could hear, whether it was because multiple people were asking or they were closest to her as she walked past she isn't sure and she isn't happy with the greetings she received.

Once she is inside away from the reporters she goes to the room where she has the exam of the Bigfoot scheduled and then checks the cooler where they have the body stored.

She finds the body undisturbed and goes to get suited up for the exam of the body.

Once her whole staff is there, she allows nobody to pass.

Juanita is angry and doesn't hide; her Mexican accent is stronger while she is speaking angrily. "Who make call to reporters? I know somebody call reporters, who made call?"

She is very demanding with her questions.

Her entire staff denies making that call.

She denies everyone entry until this is figured out.

Juanita goes to the person in charge of the facility and walks into the office unannounced.

The director is surprised to see her just walk in, "Juanita what is going on? You are not on my schedule for meeting."

Juanita has calmed down a little but her anger is still obvious. "Somebody call reporters about Bigfoot here. I have many questions and have trouble getting to door with many reporters wanting answers. I want to know who make that call to reporters. Do you know who make call?"

The director looks at her and calmly answers her, "I did, I called the reporters figuring this will help us get research funding for projects we are short on funding."

Juanita shakes her head, "How we suppose to study the Bigfoot with them out there demanding answers we don't have?"

The director leans back in her chair, "Simple, just tell them we don't have those answers yet."

Juanita, "We have not start any testing yet, so we know nothing about the Bigfoot at this time."

The director, "I am going to schedule a press conference for you, oh let's say eleven o'clock."

Juanita is surprised, "But we know nothing about the Bigfoot."

The director smiles, "Then I suppose you should get to the lab and get something to tell the reporters at the press conference."

Juanita shakes her head and walks out of the office and goes to the lab.

Juanita informs her staff about the director leaking the story about having the Bigfoot body.

Her whole staff is not in a good mood about the leak of the information.

The staff gets the body from the cooler as Juanita gets the room ready. Getting the tools out and other equipment they will be using.

The staff team moves the Bigfoots body from the gurney to the table.

One staff member takes the gurney to a different room out of the way.

Juanita gives the measurements from the large rock to a staff member that knows how to estimate the weight of the stone from the measurements. They also have the stone she brought back with her and staff members take it to weigh the stone while Juanita and others begin on the Bigfoot.

They begin with hair and blood samples for DNA testing and registration for future identification.

They move on to photographing the body and then measurements of the body.

Joe and Alex get to the house, as they enter the porch they hear a Bigfoot roar.

They don't see it and the sound is around the area they just left.

They go inside and lean the rifles in a corner and keep their pistols on their side.

They check their cell phones, since they left their phones at the house, and they both have several voicemail messages and even text messages from numbers they don't know.

They begin listening to the voicemail messages and they are from reporters wanting to know about the Bigfoot they killed and some asking for an exclusive interview.

Some reporters even offer money for an exclusive interview.

The text messages are from the same reporters making the same request they made on voicemail.

Joe and Alex are both confused how they got their numbers and how the reporters even know about the Bigfoot.

Joe calls Juanita, he wanted to call her about the bone anyway and now he has more to discuss.

Juanita has her phone turned off while she is in the lab so Joe leaves a voicemail.

Joe and Alex both listen to all their voicemails and read their text messages.

They both have a voicemail from their son Bob.

He makes the request to both of them for a return call from one of them.

He doesn't go into anything on the voicemail other than the return call request.

Alex had the least messages text and voicemail so she calls Bob back.

Bob doesn't hesitate once he sees who is calling and he answers it quickly. "Hello."

Alex, "Hello Bob, you didn't say what you were calling about. Is there something on your mind?"

Bob lets out a slight chuckle, "Mom it's being reported that you and Dad have killed a Bigfoot and that it is already at a lab in Jersey. Is that right?"

Alex is a little confused because she and Joe haven't heard anything about it on the radio they have turned on. "Where are you hearing that?"

Bob smiles as if she could see him, "It's on the news. I've seen it on the tv, haven't heard it on the radio yet."

Alex shakes her head, "We haven't turned on the tv this morning."

Bob, "So is it true?"

Alex is quiet for a moment while Joe finishes his last voice-mail. "Yes it is true."

Joe tilts his head as he looks at her.

Alex tells Bob to hold while she puts him on speaker.

Once transferred to speaker she lets him now that Joe is there as well.

Bob, "So Dad how did you manage to shoot a Bigfoot?"

Joe gives a crooked half smile, "No son, your mother killed it."

Bob's surprise is obvious in his voice, "Mom, I expected that from Dad but not from you. Sorry to assume it was you Dad."

Alex smiles while Joe responds first.

Joe, "No worries son, it surprised me as well when she came and got me to retrieve it. She didn't even tell me what she had shot. Waited until I seen it for myself."

Bob, "So Mom; what made you decide to shoot a Bigfoot?"

Alex, "Well it was actually a case of mistaken identity."

Bob is confused, "What do you mean mistaken identity? What could you have thought it was?"

Alex gives a slight shaking of her head, "Well; as odd as it sounds I thought it was a deer. A buck ran to that area in the corn and I sighted in on the deer, at least what I believed was the deer, and shot."

Bob is still confused and shakes his head, "Was the deer dark like the Bigfoot? I don't follow how you mistook a Bigfoot for a deer. Did the Bigfoot jump in front of the deer as you shot?"

Alex shakes her head like Bob could see her through the phone, "None of the above. The deer stopped on the edge of the corn where the corn was thinner and shorter. I could see enough of the deer through the corn to know it was the buck. So I raised my rifle and sighted in on it and fired, I saw it drop and then lowered the rifle and saw the buck running into the woods. I could see a body laying there on the ground and was praying it wasn't a doe that I didn't see."

Bob, "Wasn't the Bigfoot darker? I am still not understanding how you accidentally shot Bigfoot."

Alex looks at Joe and he shrugs his shoulders.

Alex, "The coloring of that Bigfoot was similar to the deer I saw. The only way I can think of how I shot it while sighting in on the buck is the Bigfoot must have moved in between the deer and myself before I got the scope on them. So I didn't know it wasn't the deer. They seemed like one being when I had the scope on them. All I saw was the deer, I couldn't tell it was anything more."

Bob, "Well, you made both of you famous. The couple who shot Bigfoot that is what the news is saying."

Alex, "Well your father and I haven't discussed doing interviews so I guess the news people will say whatever they want."

Bob, "Did you even know you became famous this morning?"

Joe and Alex answer at the same time, "No."

They finish the call with Bob and continue with the morning. They never mention anything to Bob about the Bigfoots harassing them at night. Neither of them wanted him to worry.

Joe takes his rifle and goes outside to look around and see if the Bigfoots did any more damage other than destroying the pickup.

He looks over at the wreckage that was once his pickup, but doesn't bother going over to it.

He goes into the shed and sees the corn harvester is damaged.

He walks over to it and looks at it to find out if it is still usable or if they destroyed it as well.

As he is looking at the corn harvester it appears to still be usable. All the damage appears to be cosmetic and doesn't affect its moving parts.

He looks into it more just to be sure and is satisfied that the machine will still work.

Joe walks out the opposite end of the shed, from which he entered it, where the tractor with the loader and back hoe attachments is parked.

He doesn't notice anything obviously wrong with it and walks over to it anyway to check it out to be sure.

He walks around the tractor and it looks to be unharmed so he moves to the upper floor of the barn where he has another tractor and some other equipment parked for the winter.

The barn doors are still closed and the latch is still intact so he figures they didn't get in there, unless they figured out how to work the latch.

As he goes inside the barn, again, the equipment seems to be untouched. He does notice some hay bales have been torn open and spread around.

The hay is covering everything. Not a heavy layer but enough he figures to equal two or three bales have been opened.

Since Carmen, their milk cow, wasn't in her stall to be milked this morning they had no reason to get any hay down from the hay mound. So he doesn't know if this happened overnight or while he and Alex were looking for Carmen.

Joe decides not to begin cleaning up the mess from the broken hay bales and instead decides to investigate the hay mound.

He finds six strings that were holding the bales together and now he knows that he has three bales scattered around the barn floor.

He found those strings at the base of the ladder going to the hay mound.

He continues and climbs the ladder to the top of the hay stacked in the mound.

Joe looks around and then walks onto the hay and around the stack looking to see if more is missing.

He knows how he and Alex usually remove hay as they need it and he knows how the stack was when he retrieved the last bale for Carmen while they milked her.

He notices where more than three bales have been removed from a different area of the stack.

He walks over to that area and he counts seven missing bales.

He can account for three scattered around the barn floor so that leaves four unaccounted for.

He also notices a foul odor in that area of the stack.

He puts his rifle to his shoulder keeping the barrel pointing down as he looks around the hay stack and around the barn from the top of the stack.

He sees hair on the hay. He figures it must be Bigfoot hair because there is no other reason for the hair to be laying on top of the hay like it is.

He doesn't see any evidence of a Bigfoot hiding in the hay or anywhere in the barn that he can see. The odor as well isn't real strong like there would be one close but faint like it is a residual odor from one that left.

He decides not to bend over to sniff the hay or the hair to verify that the odor is there and not a Bigfoot hiding.

Joe decides he would prefer to keep his breakfast down and not make himself sick before lunch.

Joe climbs down out of the hay mound and walks outside then closes the doors and latches them again before moving on around the area.

He walks around the barn on the side that is overgrown because it hasn't been maintained for years. He has broken equipment that he can't get parts for and some he has for the parts so he can keep his usable equipment running, parked in that area of the property.

He can see where something has been going through the high weeds, grass and brush.

He decides to walk the path that is there to see what is in there or at least where the path leads.

He finds an area outside the window in the bottom of the barn that they keep open where the vegetation is crushed. Like someone or something was crouched or perhaps laying there.

He can see the path continues towards the pasture.
Joe stops to look at the barn around the window and notices hair stuck in the frame around the open window.

He kneels down out of the window and realizes there is a gap between the boards of the barn wall. He can see straight into the stall where Carmen was milked every day and he can even see the door where he and Alex enter and leave.

Again he can smell the faint odor of the Bigfoot which makes him believe a Bigfoot watched them as they entered and left and while they milked the cow.

Needless to say Joe isn't happy learning that they were being watched.

Now he is wondering how long they were being watched.

He stands back up and continues following the path toward the pasture.

He finds two bales of hay tossed into the vegetation, one to each side of the path.

He figures a Bigfoot tossed them but is surprised that they didn't toss them farther of the path.

He walks the rest of the path to the pasture and doesn't see the other two missing bales of hay.

From the ending of the path he can see a used path through the pasture toward the trees where Alex's tree stand was located. It appears to be a well-used path.

He never noticed the path before, but from the angle he is looking at it now it is an obvious path. It appears to be a very well-used path.

He can see remnants of hay that feel from the bales as they were carried across the pasture.

Again he isn't sure when it happened and he decides to count the cattle in the pasture just to be sure none were taken like Carmen.

He walks into the pasture and counts the cattle.

The herd is all accounted for so he returns to the hay bales left along the trail.

He puts his rifle over his back so he can carry the bales back to the barn.

He retrieves the bales from the vegetation and then takes one in each hand and carries them back to the barn using the path he found.

Joe hears movement in the vegetation but doesn't see anything, but then again the vegetation is as tall as and even taller than he is in places.

Joe gets to the doors of the barn and puts the bales down so he can open the doors.

Again he hears movement in the tall vegetation but doesn't see anything, he can't even see the vegetation moving so figures it must be a smaller animal like a groundhog perhaps a raccoon.

So he continues opening the barn doors and not worrying about the movement. He knows birds nest in that vegetation and they can also be very noisy when moving around in there.

He opens the doors and puts the hay bales inside next to the hay mound on the floor figuring on using those the next time he needs hay.

He turns and sees a Bigfoot standing in the opening of the doors and then it runs from the open doors, after realizing it has been seen, toward the path in the tall vegetation.

Joe didn't even have time to reach for a firearm let alone get a shot.

He removes his rifle from his back and moves toward the doors slowly staying to one side of the barn allowing him a line of sight in the direction it ran. Hopefully to see it before it can attack him.

Joe gets to the doors and the creature is nowhere in sight.

Joe moves outside slowly and moving his gaze and rifle quickly in each direction checking for a Bigfoot so he is not surprised by one. But again he sees nothing.

Joe puts his rifle over his shoulder and closes the barn doors and latches them again.

He then removes his rifle from his shoulder and walks toward the house, it is almost noon now. He has spent the last few hours looking around the buildings and machinery on the farm looking for other damage. But his pickup is the most damaged piece of equipment of anything on the farm including the damage to the house which he looks up at as he walks to the house and thinks to himself about needing to finish that job today.

He walks inside the house and Alex has lunch almost ready.

Alex asks what he found while walking around.

Joe tells her about the hay bales missing, the ones he found and about the bales broken and spread inside the barn.

She asks about the farm equipment.

He tells her the only thing not usable is the pickup.

She shows some relieve that the other equipment is still usable.

Alex sets lunch on the table and they sit down to eat.

Alex tells Joe that Jane (their daughter) called while he was outside.

Joe looks at her, "Oh, what is on her mind today?"

Alex smiles, "Well you know, the same reason Bob called, about the news reports."

Before Joe responds to Alex his phone is ringing.

He looks at the phone to see who it is and it is Juanita returning his call.

Joe tells Alex who is calling and he answers the call and puts it on speaker so Alex can hear as well.

Joe answers with no emotion in his voice, "Hello."

Juanita sounds vaguely apologetic but not fully, "Joe, this Juanita return you call. You say you have bone with teeth marks on it?"

Joe, "Yes, it is a bone from our dairy cow. We believe the cow was carried away because we saw no sign of the cow being dragged and no sign of the cow being killed in the barn. Our cow was weighing over one thousand pounds."

Juanita doesn't sound surprised, "That is interesting Joe. The stone you show us on the fence we estimate at one thousand five hundred pounds and the stone you carry to us it weigh one hundred fifty pounds. So a cow no problem for them to carry."

Joe asks her if she wants the bone sent to her.

Juanita agrees and gives him the mailing address so he can mail it to her.

Joe allows curiosity into his voice and not anger, "We have both gotten calls from reporters about the Bigfoot you got from us yesterday. We don't know how they got our numbers or the information about the Bigfoot at all."

Juanita now has a fully apologetic voice, "I sorry, my supervisor she release you numbers to reporters without me knowing. She tell me today after I come in with many reporters outside asking questions I no have answers for. I had to talk to them hour ago and answer questions that I could answer. But I say nothing about you or Alex."

Alex, "Sorry to hear your supervisor couldn't keep it secret long enough for you to even study it."

Joe, "Did you even look at the creature, scientifically, yesterday after you got back to the lab?"

Juanita shakes her head, "No, we look at it this morning only. Still much to learn from it."

Joe informs Juanita about the Bigfoots destroying the pickup and not destroying anything else.

Juanita suggests it may be because the dead one was in the back of the pickup and had its scent. The others could have been looking to see if it was there or destroyed the pickup because it held the dead one for the night.

Joe agrees with her thought about them destroying the pickup because it held the dead one overnight. He then tells her that he was thinking that as well because other Bigfoots tried to stop her from leaving with the dead one so they must know it left the area.

They talk a little while longer, Joe lets her know the Bigfoots in the area are still watching them and has taken bales of hay. Juanita suggests that might be for bedding. Joe and Alex agree considering nobody knows if the creatures eat hay themselves.

They end the call and Joe and Alex get the bone boxed up and addressed for shipping then get in the car and go to town to mail the package.

Upon returning to the house they notice one of the solar lights that Alex put up was down and destroyed.

They park the car and walk around the side of the house and realize all the solar lights she put up are down and destroyed.

Some of them are sunk into the ground inside of a large footprint with the light in pieces.

Alex, "So now if we leave they will destroy something else?"

Joe shakes his head, "I don't know babe. But it looks like they are getting rid of the lights nearest to the house."

Alex, "So they can get closer without being seen, just great."

Joe looks at her, "Do we have any solar lights left?"

Alex thinks before answering, "I believe we had two or three left and don't know if there are more than that."

Joe smiles, "Good enough, let's get those remaining lights up and take back the area with light."

Alex smiles and she goes to the storage shed for the remaining lights while Joe gets the ladder.
They meet up where Alex had put the first light.
It's three o'clock now and they will soon be out of daylight so they work as fast as possible to get the three lights up that Alex had found.

The dogs are playing in the yard without showing any concern.

Joe puts the ladder up on the side of a tree and Alex has the first light open and the mounting hardware ready to hand to him.

Joe goes up the ladder with the tools and Alex hands him the pieces of mounting hardware as he is ready for them.

They hear several Bigfoot roars beginning around Alex's deer stand and all around them even to Joe's stand.

Joe looks around from the ladder and doesn't see any signs of the creatures in any direction.

The dogs have stopped playing and are sitting on guard next to Alex.

The German Shepard turns to a far corner of the house from them and stands and starts growling, the Husky moves next to the Shepard and begins growling as well while looking in the same direction.

Joe and Alex both look but don't see anything.

They look at each other and shrug their shoulders and go back to work.

The dogs keep their attention on that corner of the house as Joe and Alex finish that light and move to the next position.

Joe is trying to cover as much area with the three lights as possible. He is hoping to provide enough light to discourage the Bigfoots from coming in from that area.

Joe puts the ladder up at the second location for a light that is closer to that corner the dogs are watching.

The dogs will not go to the corner but continue to growl.

Joe goes up the ladder and again Alex hands him the material as he needs it.

While they are putting the light up the dogs change their attention to the corner of the house closer to the previous light. Again Joe and Alex see nothing, but now they are getting the distinct odor of a Bigfoot. It isn't strong but definitely noticeable.

They get that light mounted and move around the house and begin installing the last light.

As they finish the last light and begin gathering everything to put away they hear a Bigfoot roar and it is close, they both cover their ears.

Chapter 9
INTENTIONS REVEALED

The dogs even tried to hide when the Bigfoot roared, but ended up hiding behind Joe and Alex and working their heads between Joe and Alex's legs to protect their ears. The German Shepard tried hiding between Alex's legs and the Husky between Joe's legs.

Once the roar ends they uncover their ears and the dogs stay between their legs for a short time, at least until Joe and Alex start to move to finish putting everything away.

Joe and Alex don't say anything about the roar because they both suspect that was the one the dogs were warning them about being close while installing the lights.

As they are putting away the tools and ladder they hear more roars and howls all around them.

Joe sees Alex reaching for her rifle and tells her not to reach for a firearm.

She looks at him like he is nuts, "Why?"

Joe, "Because we can't see them and don't know their intent at this time. Besides if they are intelligent creatures maybe just maybe they will understand we don't mean them harm as long as they don't threaten us."

Alex shakes her head, "I still think you are nuts. They are animals; nobody has any proof of their intentions towards humans. But we now know they will attack and destroy property."

They begin walking back to the house as Joe responds, "But we; well you." He smiles as he looks at her, "Killed one first and apparently angered them to the point they retaliated."

Alex stops and her anger is obvious in her voice, "Hold on, you saying this is all my fault?"

Joe turns and looks at her, "No babe, not at all. It could have as easily been me killing one if it would have gotten between me and my target without me knowing it. Especially one like you shot and the hair color is similar to what I am shooting at. I'm not blaming you for any of this; as far as I am concerned we are in this together and we will get through this together."

Alex hugs him, "Thank you."

They continue to the house and go inside.

Joe, "Remember some of the stories we have found on the internet recently babe? The stories that tell about not showing aggression toward the Bigfoot and it/they won't be aggressive. I believe it is worth trying; don't you?"

Alex shakes her head, "I do remember those stories but do you remember the stories about the ones that are aggressive for no reason. Not to mention the people that have been hunted by the Bigfoot after shooting at one let alone killing one?"

Joe nods his head, "Yes babe, but don't you think we should at least try to make peace with the creatures? If we don't make peace and live together they could easily run us into financial ruin by killing the cattle, destroying our farm equipment. That's if they don't just up and kill us by hitting us with a stone while we have our back to them not knowing they're there."

Alex looks at him, "I suppose you want us to go outside and face in the direction of one of the creatures and hold our hands out to show we are not armed and tell them that we mean them no harm and we want to share the property with them peacefully. I suppose you believe that will work like that one individual suggested to someone else online. After the one admitted to being watched by the creatures for thirty years, I think it was, after he had killed two of them he said. Thirty years honey those things stalked that person. Do you really expect they will leave us alone if we do what that guy told the one being stalked to do?"

Joe shrugs his shoulders, "I don't know babe, but if we don't try they may continue to destroy equipment, kill cattle God only knows what they would do."

Alex shakes her head, "I still say what I have said for many years now. You're a blooming idiot, but you're my idiot and I still love you."

Joe hugs her, "I still love you even though you're a smarty pants."

They both laugh and exchange a kiss.

They agree to go outside and try what they have heard online about facing in the direction of the creatures and showing that they are not armed. Then telling the Bigfoots that they want to live in peace with them.

They leave the firearms inside and go across the pasture toward the area they hear the most vocalizations come from.

They put their arms straight out and talk to the woods telling any creature within the sound of their voices that they mean no harm and want to live in peace with them. They tell the creatures the area is big enough for us all to live in peace. Nobody else needs to get hurt or killed on either side. They even mention that the first one was an accident and the others were because they felt the need to protect themselves.

They hear grunts, whistles, and even a roar that again gets responses from all round them.

Alex looks around as the others respond to the one closer to them. "Do you think that means they understand and will agree to live in peace?"

Joe puts his arm around Alex and looks around as well, "I don't know babe, we can only hope and pray to God that they understand and will agree."

Alex nods her head as they turn to walk back to the house, "Hopefully that dude we heard online knows what he was talking about and that these ones will follow the behavior patterns he expects from them."

Joe agrees, "The guy seemed to know what he was talking about but like you said these ones would have to behave as he expects."

They get back to the house and have heard nothing more from anywhere on the property.

They go inside and remember they don't need to milk tonight since the Bigfoot creatures took Carmen.

They do the other evening chores and then have supper and do their usual nightly routine watching tv and relaxing.

The dogs are with them laying at their feet on the living room floor.

The night is quiet, the dogs go outside for their potty break before bed and show no signs of concern and even play a little after they take care of their business.

Alex gets the coffee pot ready for morning while Joe stands on the back porch while the dogs are in the yard.

Joe and the dogs come in and everyone goes upstairs to go to bed.

Alex, "Do you think we can trust the creatures to leave us

alone tonight?"

Joe tilts his head to one side with a shoulder shrug, "I don't know but they have been good so far tonight and I guess we will find out."

They take their pistols to bed with them as a precaution and place them on the night stand on their respective side of the bed.

The pistols are loaded and in the holsters to prevent any accidents.

They go to bed and all is quiet as they fall asleep.

About one o'clock in the morning the solar motion lights turn on and the dogs don't even notice the lights.

The lights go out without anyone inside realizing they were even activated.

The Bigfoot that activated the light quickly ran away from the light as it and others looked at the light and figured out when the light would come on.

The Bigfoots then stayed where they wouldn't trigger the solar motion lights and had a younger one reach up and remove the lights while standing on an adult's shoulders.

The young Bigfoot quickly ran back into the woods after the lights were removed and an adult destroyed each solar light.

The Bigfoot creatures begin looking in the windows.

They don't see anyone downstairs so one jumps onto the porch roof and the dogs hear it land on the roof and begin barking.

Joe and Alex wake up and shine a flashlight around outside through a window and don't see anything in the light beam from the flashlight.

Joe walks around with his flashlight and pistol in hand, removed from the holster, into each room that has a window to the porch roof.

He enters each room slowly, keeping the lights off including his flashlight, as he looks around the room and out the window.

They left the outside porch light on and it is providing some light that Joe can see around without his flashlight.

He can't see every detail but can make out shapes and if he is to see something that shouldn't be on the roof then he will use the flashlight. But he doesn't see anything that would be cause for concern and doesn't use his flashlight to look around from the other windows.

He also notices the solar lights are not on and figures a Bigfoot threw something and the dogs heard it land but he didn't since he was asleep.

Joe can't see the light fixtures in the dark anyway and takes it for granted nothing is there since the lights are not on.

Joe returns to bed and when Alex asks if he seen anything he simply responses with a no.

Joe doesn't doubt the dogs heard or seen something but figures their barking scared it away.

The dogs lay back down when Joe does and they all go back to sleep.

When the dogs barked after the Bigfoot landed on the porch roof the Bigfoot jumped down and they all ran into the darkness away from the house.

The Bigfoots are hiding in the darkness away from the house and waiting.

They are waiting for all movement to stop inside.

It is now three o'clock and the Bigfoots start to move in towards the house again.

One goes ahead and listens carefully but doesn't hear any movement so it makes a low volume grunt and the others come in closer.

One of them climbs onto the porch roof this time and is able to stay quiet enough not to wake the dogs.

It moves around looking inside each window it comes to and when it sees Joe and Alex in bed it backs away from the window quickly. Just enough to be out of the window and it listens for movement and doesn't hear any movement so it peeks around slowly and then sees the dogs sleeping on the floor.

The Bigfoot doesn't move and just watches the dogs and the people, only moving its eyes and not its head as it changes who it is looking at.

After a few minutes it lets out a low volume grunt as it watches the occupants inside.

The dogs moved but didn't wake, the humans never moved.

The other Bigfoots are moving towards doors and windows.

A few more climb up onto the porch roof.

A Bigfoot on the porch lets out a grunt a little louder than the other two did.

All the Bigfoots are entering the house, breaking through

doors and windows.

They are inside before anyone woke up.

The dogs realize what is inside and they run and hide.

There were two Bigfoot creatures that entered the bedroom from separate windows and have Joe and Alex before they knew what was happening.

Joe and Alex never had a chance to reach for their pistols.

The Bigfoots carry Joe and Alex away from the house and into the woods.

Juanita goes to get into her car to leave for work and finds her car destroyed, smashed beyond recognition.

She knows it's her car because it's where she parks her car regularly.

The cars next to her on either side weren't damaged, not even a new scratch.

Juanita calls the police and they arrive and admit they have never seen anything like that before.

Over at Steve's apartment complex he finds the exact same thing has happened to his car and the cars next to his weren't damaged.

Steve calls the police and he is told the same thing that they told Juanita.

Granted it was different officers at each call but had same verbal response as to never seeing anything like that before.

Steve is able to get a taxi to get to work and is late.

Juanita is late as well and had also called a taxi to get to work.

They get to the building about the same time and it looked like it was hit by a tornado, and that was the only building hit.

The director stops Juanita and asks if she knows what happened last night.

Before Juanita answers there are two officers standing there as well asking the same question.

Juanita plainly says she has no idea what happened.

Steve is close by and mentions how it reminds him of his car this morning.

Juanita looks at him, "What you mean look like you car?"

Steve tells her what his car looked like this morning and

shows her pictures of it.

The director is looking as well.

Juanita has a surprised look, "My car same this morning."

She shows pictures of her car as well.

The director mentions the other cars do not look damaged.

They look at the director and answer at the same time, "The other cars were not damaged."

Juanita and Steve look at each other with a similar thought.

Juanita speaks first, "It look intentional and only one car target. Other cars ok no damage."

Steve agrees it looked intentional on the one car.

Steve looks at the director and asks if anything is missing inside the building.

The director says they haven't been inside yet the officers haven't finished clearing the building.

Juanita looks at Steve, "You no think, maybe they take the dead and kill our cars."

Steve nods his head, "That is my thought at this time. I don't know how else to explain the damage to the building or our cars. The building doors look like something went through them."

The officers haven't left yet and the ranking officer asks, "What are you talking about?"

Steve calmly states, "Bigfoot. I believe multiple Bigfoot creatures attacked last night and took the dead one from inside and destroyed our cars because we brought the dead one here."

The officers laugh.

Juanita nods her head agreeing with his theory.

The lower ranked officer, "You mean this is the place that has the dead Bigfoot? Now you think they are smart enough to co-ordinate an attack in three places at once."

Again the officers laugh.

The officers that were searching the building come out and give the all clear.

The director asks Juanita and Steve to wait, and the director goes to the highest ranking officer on site.

A short discussion and the director returns and shortly after the two officers and two higher ranking officers join them.

The director looks at Juanita and Steve, "These four officers will escort you to your lab so you can verify if the specimen is still in the cooler or if it has been stolen. I am heading to security to check the video surveillance from the night. We have a guard in the hospital in critical condition and I would like to know what happened here."

Juanita, Steve and their escorts walk toward the lab.

The place is a total mess, the tornado hit inside as well as outside.

Broken glass and holes in the walls, doors broken off the hinges and some doors have just been totally splintered.

They get to their lab and it is no different. It is totally destroyed, very expensive equipment destroyed and the door to the cooler is gone.

They see that door on the other side of the lab and where it hit the wall hard enough that it is stuck in the wall.

They look inside the cooler and realize the body is gone.

The gurney it was on is crushed.

Steve looks at the officers, "What were you saying about their intelligence?"

The officers don't respond.

Juanita looks at Steve and places her hand on his arm, "Steve, that no change what happen here. We need to study what we still have and learn what we can."

Steve looks at her, "I know you're right."

They continue helping the rest of the staff put together a list of what is missing to for the police report.

The director has two officers go with her to the security office so they can retrieve the recording from last night.

They see the imprint in the wall where the guard's body hit the wall.

One of the officers looks at the imprint, "Holy cow what hit there?"

They go inside the guard's office and the director gets access into the nights recordings.

They begin with outside and at one o'clock they see multiple Bigfoots enter into the video and go straight for the door.

Then they go to interior video at the door and see a Bigfoot smash its way through the door.

The younger of the two officers, "Holy crap is that a Bigfoot?"

The director never looks away from the screen, "No sir that is many

Bigfoots."

The other officer just looks at the first one, "Just watch."

The younger officer nods in agreeance.

They keep watching the video and changing cameras as needed to keep tract of the movement of the creatures.

They watch as the Bigfoot creatures break through door after door and destroy each room they enter into.

The director is wondering why they haven't seen the security guard yet.

Then the director finds the video and sees the time stamp on the video.

One of the creatures apparently went straight to the guard's office and smashed through the door and the guard used his Taser on the creature and had no effect.

Then the guard used his pepper spray and made good contact with the creature's eyes.

As that one is screaming in pain the guard didn't see the other one come in since he was watching the one in pain and not watching the door.

The second one had the guard by the neck and threw him into the wall in the hallway before he ever knew he was grabbed.

The creature picked the guard up and threw him with one hand. The guard is weighing in at an even two hundred pounds as the director pointed out to the officers.

Both officers are surprised.

They keep watching as they group moves through the building.

The two that attacked the guard are moving again after the one recovers from the pepper spray and they head straight to the lab with where the dead one is being examined.

The director notices that it looks like the one that wasn't sprayed is using its nose and sniffing the air. The only thing the director can think about is it can smell the other one and is following the odor.

The director doesn't say anything to the officers and waits to see if they notice.

The creatures get to the lab and break through the door and the one that was sprayed follows the other one as it sniffs its way to the cooler.

It grabs the door and rips it from the frame.

Not all the hinges stayed on the frame some stayed attached to the door.

The creature throws the door across the room and they watch as the door is planted in the wall from the force used to throw it.

The one goes inside the cooler and lets out a roar that shakes the camera.

Others come into the room as the dead one is carried out of the cooler.

The director is watching the movements of the creatures and notices what she believes to be the display of grief.

Then the audio sound that is recorded she believes it sounds sad, depressing and has her thinking it is them verbally grieving for the dead.

The older officer asks if they can get a copy of the video for the report.

The director agrees and tells the officer that she will have the next guard forward the recording as soon as he can.

The officer agrees and gives her an email address to forward the video before the officers leave her.

The director calls Juanita by cell phone and asks her to report to the guard office to watch the video.

Juanita arrives and the director shows her the video and asks if she would have figured any of it from the creature's strength to its compassion for another creature.

Juanita admits she would not have estimated its strength to that degree and would not have figured the compassion at all. Then adds that is why they need to be studied.

The director asks who would be crazy enough to be close enough to study them for the amount of time that would be needed.

Juanita simply replies she don't know and that she believes someone will.

The director laughs a little, "It will probably be a twenty something year old looking to make a name for themselves and if they don't kill the individual than that person would become very famous."

Juanita agrees.

The next shift of guard arrives and the director gives him the email address to the officer and stays to make sure the email is sent to her as well in a separate email.

The guard emails the complete video to the officers and then to the director.

Juanita had already went back to the lab and is again cleaning up the mess and figuring out what equipment is still usable and what is worthless.

The director goes to her office and on the way gets a call on her cell phone from the hospital.

The guard that was attacked died on the operating table, his injuries were too severe and he had a lot of internal bleeding.

The director thanks the nurse for the call and continues to her office.

Once in her office she looks up the number to the guard's family and calls them to inform them of his passing.

The director didn't want them finding out on the news.

The guard's wife asks what happened.

The director explains what happened.

The guard's wife, needless to say, is very emotional. She is grief stricken and angry at the lab for bringing such a dangerous creature into the building.

The director explains that there was no way of knowing that the creatures would break into the building or kill anyone. She continues and explains there was no way of knowing just how strong the creatures are either, that is why the studies are so important.

The guard's wife doesn't respond she just hangs up.

Juanita and her staff find many of their samples have survived so they can at least perform some of their experiments to map the DNA of the creature. As well as some of the other tests they wanted to do with blood and hair samples.

They still have their measurements of the Bigfoot and with the video evidence they will try to estimate the strength of the creature so they can hopefully capture a living specimen for study.

Juanita thinks to call Joe later in the morning and gets his voicemail and leaves a message for him to call her back. She includes that the lab was broken into by the creatures and they took the dead one last night and the guard was attacked and not expected to live.

Juanita and the rest of the personnel in the building haven't been updated as yet that the guard has died.

Chapter 10
SELL THE FARM

Bod and Jane both have called their parents several times through the day and have not received a return call.

Juanita has not received a return call either, but she isn't concerned since she has always gotten a return call when they had the time.

The third day with not hearing from Joe or Alex, Bob calls the neighbor to check on them.

The neighbor gets to the house and notices the doors and windows broken into the house.

The neighbor calls the police before going inside.

The dogs come out to greet the neighbor.

The neighbor asks the dogs where Joe and Alex are at and the dogs look towards the pasture to the area where Alex had her tree stand.

The neighbor looks that direction but doesn't see them and figures he isn't understanding the dogs.

While waiting for the police he notices the pickup, at least what he believed was the pickup.

He calls Bob back and informs him as to what was found and that the police are on the way.

Bob tells the neighbor that he is coming out as well.

Bob calls his sister and lets her know and she decides to go to the house as well.

Bob and Jane arrive in separate vehicles and at the same time, barely slowing down for the turn into the driveway.

The neighbor is already talking to a police officer.

Bob and Jane go to run straight into the house and officers catch them and stop them from running inside.

The officers tell them there are officers inside the house searching it now and if they just run inside without it being announced they could be hurt.

The officers tell them that they are making sure there isn't anyone inside that would attack as well as searching for Joe and Alex.

Jane's emotions are obvious in her voice, "This is our parent's house, is our parents ok? What happened here, are they ok?" She is fighting the urge to cry.

One of the officers not holding them tells them again that they have officers inside conducting a search of the house and we will all know more when they come out.

The dogs go to Bob and Jane.

Bob and Jane both agree to the officer that they will wait until the others come out with their report of what is inside.

Jane begins talking to the dogs while petting them.

She asks when they were feed last and what happened to Mom and Dad.

The dogs look toward the area Alex's tree stand was located.

The neighbor points out to her that the dogs looked in that direction when he asked about Joe and Alex as well.

Bob asks if he has gone down there to check out the area at all.

The neighbor says he has not.

The officers come out of the house.

Bob and Jane are there as they go the ranking officer on site. The neighbor stays back but is close enough to hear.

The officers tell that the house is empty.

There is nobody inside, and aside from the broken doors and windows there is no evidence of foul play.

J   ane looks at the officers not caring who answers, "So what does that mean?"

The ranking officer, "That means that we have no evidence of a crime beyond forced entry and without the home owners we have nobody to file the complaint to investigate."

Bob speaks up, "We are the children," pointing to Jane and himself, "of the homeowners and we would like to file the report for investigation."

The officer takes his and Jane's information and they also file a missing person's report while they are filing with the police.

The officer accepts that nobody has seen or heard from Joe or Alex in three days and puts that in the missing person's report.

They hear and sound that none of them are familiar with.

It is a Bigfoot roar from the area of Alex's tree stand and another from the area of Joe's tree stand.

But nobody there knows those are Bigfoot roars since they

haven't been around to understand.

The neighbor does mention he has heard that sound from this area for a few nights and then the last three nights he hasn't heard the sounds.

Bob mentions that the sounds came from Mom and Dad's tree stand, at least in that area.

Bob asks Jane if she would check Mom's stand and he will check Dad's stand.

Jane agrees.

The ranking officer tells them to hold on and not rush out there.

Jane tells him that those sounds could be from her parent's and they could be hurt.

The officer agrees but adds that he will send two officers with each of them in case it is whoever did this to the house.

Bob and Jane agree and head to the stands with their escorts.

The neighbor starts talking to the officer and asks if he believes in Bigfoot.

The officer laughs and says no.

The neighbor, "Well this is the farm where they proved it exists. The couple that lives here are the ones in the news that killed one."

The officer looks at him with a look of not knowing whether to believe him or not.

They continue with small talk and the neighbor lets it known he has heard gun shots after dark at this house a few nights ago.

The officer asks if he reported it to the game commission as poaching isn't his area of investigation.

The neighbor laughs and tells the officer they weren't known to be poachers even when they desperately needed the meat.

Jane and her escorts are running back to the house as fast as they all can run.

There is gun shots from Joe's tree stand area and Bob is running as fast as he can with no escorts.

They hear a blood curdling scream that sounds human in nature from the area of Joe's stand, only the one scream.

They all get back to the house and the ranking officer is demanding to know what is going on and what happened.

Jane's escorts speak up at the same time then one allows the other to tell what happened.

Officer, "Sir, you won't believe this but we were chased out by Bigfoot. More than one came at us, some with logs and others with bare hands."

The ranking officer looks at Bob.

Bob, "Same for us, except they surprised us and the officers told me to run while they hold them back."

They hear another roar which is followed by several more surrounding them.

The ranking officer calls in for more officers.

Bob mentions the firearms inside if nobody stole them.

They go inside and Bob gets the keys to the gun safe.

Bob grabs Joe's 25-06.

Jane takes the 30-30.

The neighbor is offered the 30-06 but turns it down.

Bob asks if he is a hunter and the neighbor replies that he hunts but has heard that if no aggression is shown to the Bigfoot they in turn will not be aggressive. The neighbor adds that since his farm is the next property he would prefer to try for peace with the creatures.

The officers went to their cruisers to retrieve their rifles.

They come outside and Bob mentions about the pistols being missing.

One of the officers that searched the house mentions two pistols upstairs in the bedroom on the night stands next to the bed and loaded.

Bob runs back inside and gets the pistols from the bedroom.

After Bob comes back out he hands the 357 to Jane and he puts the 44 on his side.

They hear a roar that is loud enough that they feel it; they all cover their ears as well.

The dogs take off and hide.

One of the officers points into the hay field. "It's up there."

They all look and there is a Bigfoot standing on the hill looking down at them.

It is between five hundred to six hundred yards away.

Bob raises the rifle.

The ranking officer puts his hand on the barrel and pushes it down.

Bob is angry, "Why would you do that, I can easily make that shot. Dad and I are close enough the way we shoot I could get a killing shot."

The officer doesn't say a word just points and moves his hand as he is pointing all the way around them.

Bob follows the officer's hand as he points to all the creatures that are now in plain view.

The creatures are several hundred yards away and have the humans greatly outnumbered.

They all know that they can't shoot fast enough to drop every Bigfoot before they would be on top of them. If the creatures decide to charge.

Nobody raises a rifle towards a single creature.

They all stand and stare at each other for five minutes that feel like five hours to the humans.

Finally the creatures all retreat back to the trees and disappear as they enter the tree line.

The officers wait for their back up to arrive so they can go search for the other two officers and hopefully recover them alive or at least their bodies to take back.

The neighbor tells Bob and Jane to let him know what they find out about Joe and Alex.

Bob and Jane agree and thank him for his help and willingness to check on their parents.

The neighbor asks what they will do with the farm and the livestock.

Bob and Jane agree it will all most likely be sold.

The neighbor tells them he will check on the cattle until they sell the heard if they would like him to do that.

Bob and Jane agree and thank him again.

The neighbor goes home.

Bob and Jane go inside and look around.

The creatures destroyed the refrigerator and ate the food. But they assume the dogs ate some as well since the door was off and they were not feed for three days that they know of.

The house smells of the creatures but they don't know the creature's odor and just think the house stinks.

They find their parents cell phones and plug them in to charge.

Once they have enough of a charge to turn on the check the phones for missed calls and messages.

They see Juanita's name for a message and several missed

calls.

Bob calls her back.

Juanita is happy to see Joe's number calling her, "Joe, where you been? You no call for many day now."

Bob, "Sorry miss Juanita. This is Bob Joe's son. Dad and Mom are missing and we don't know what happened."

Juanita's voice gets sorrowful, "I sorry, how the house look when you get there?"

Bob isn't sure what to think about the question, "It was trashed; doors and windows broken into the house like someone came in through them."

Juanita, "You know you Mom and Dad kill Bigfoot yes?"

Bob smiles a little, "Yes."

Juanita, "I came and take the Bigfoot from them to the lab in New Jersey. The lab was attacked three day ago. When I no more get to talk to you Dad. The lab was broke in the same way, we had a guard killed by Bigfoot and they take the dead one away, it all on video."

Bob nods his head, "I believe it, we just had more Bigfoot creatures show themselves to us as a show of force than I think most people would believe exist as a whole population."

Juanita, "Yes many came inside the lab to get the dead one out."

Bob looks surprised, "The one Mom killed or did you have another one?"

Juanita looks a little surprised at the question, "We only had one, the one you Mom kill."

Bob, "But you transported it from here in Pennsylvania to New Jersey; many miles away from the farm where it was killed. You are in the city as well and they would have had to show themselves in the city."

Juanita hasn't thought about it like that, "You right, many miles away it was killed. They came in at one o'clock in the morning and not many people to see them that time of morning."

Bob shakes his head still not understanding why the creatures would travel so far to get one of their dead. Then he thinks about it differently and asks Juanita, "Do you think, instead of them following you from here. How about they called out and followed you vocally and then had creatures in that area go in and get the body back."

Juanita thinks about his theory, "You might have good thought. I do not know about the Bigfoot to say if they would do like you think or not."

Bob, "Well I better let you go. I am sure you have a lot of work to do. I still need to find Dad's truck. Unless they used it and left the farm."

Juanita, "Oh no they no use the truck, it look like my car. You Dad send me picture of it after it happen. It smashed and look like pile of junk now, like my car."

Bob is confused again, "Wait, you mean the creatures crushed the truck and your car?"

Juanita smiles slightly, "Yes, only way to explain is the Bigfoot crush the car and you Dad truck. Picture of truck and my car in you Dad phone, we send to each other."

Bob, "Ok I will look at them. Thank you for the talk."

Juanita smiles, "You welcome. Oh You Dad send me bone of cow that was eaten. We check the teeth marks on the bone and Bigfoot eat the cow. Not the exact one we had here dead but marks close enough to be a Bigfoot eat the cow."

Bob, "Thank you, we still need to walk around the farm and see what we need to do yet."

They end their call and Bob checks the messages with Juanita's name. Then checks the pictures sent between them and sees the pictures of the truck and her car.

Bob tells Jane about the truck and they go outside and find the pile of metal that was once the truck.

They decide to go home.

Bob has made a list of needed repairs.

Jane takes the dogs, the dog food that was still there and the dog's food bowls.

The ranking state trooper had assured them that they will organize and conduct a search of the surrounding area.

The officer's backup has arrived and they all go searching for the missing officers.

They go into the woods in a line keeping in sight of each other as they move through the woods.

An officer shouts out he found a gun belt.

Another officer shouts out she found another gun belt.

They mark the location on gps and continue the search and

find the officers badges and pieces of bloody clothing.

They again mark the area on gps and what was found at the location.

They search until almost dark and do not find the missing officers, not even any blood except what was on the clothing they found.

The search is called off for the night.

The next morning the officers arrive with the state game commission officers and many volunteers to conduct the search for Joe, Alex and the two missing officers.

Bob and Jane are there as well without their families.

The state police and the local game commission officer are coordinating their search and have groups assigned to search in a grid pattern.

Bob and Jane join in the search.

The day wears on with no evidence of any of the missing.

The previous night with the materials found of the two officers the search party was hopeful of at least finding one or both of them, even if they have died.

The search is called again due to the darkness of night and scheduled to resume the next morning.

The next five days have the same results with no evidence being found of the missing.

The searchers do hear Bigfoot roars and some are close enough to hear growls and grunts.

One day a searcher surprised a Bigfoot and it screamed as it ran away.

The searcher was a non-believer and after that encounter he not only believed but also had to change his underwear.

The search is called off after two weeks and no other evidence was found of the missing. A few volunteers continued searching on their own for another three days and then they too gave up.

Bob has had carpenters at the house to do the needed repairs including the exterior wall.

Bob and Jane have gotten the place cleaned up and ready to sell.

They have divided their parent's belongings and have made an agreement with the neighbor for the herd of cattle.

The neighbor also took the barn cats to his place to catch mice since he had no barn cats.

They have an auction scheduled to sell the belongings they didn't take and have the farm listed with a realtor to sell.

Auction day comes and goes well.

Nobody saw a Bigfoot but several were heard through the day and most people didn't know what the sound was from, only a few folks knew the sound was a Bigfoot.

Several weeks go by and the realtor is showing the farm to potential buyers.

Many people are interested but only one couple decided to buy it for a working farm.

Bob and Jane had agreed not to sell the farm to a developer that would buy it just to sell it by the lot and have many houses built in a close proximity to each other. Making it a small town and no longer a working farm.

There was a few of them that looked at the farm and some even offered cash money without financing the amount.

One developer even doubled the asking price in cash and they still refused to sell to him.

He admitted that he heard about the Bigfoot killed on the farm and was going to call the development Bigfoot Acres and use the whole story to sell lots.

The couple that bought the farm was a young couple just starting their lives together.

They both grew up on a farm and wanted a farm of their own after they got married.

Bob and Jane wish them the best of luck when they sign the paperwork.

There was no mention of the Bigfoot on the property. But the young couple are from the local area and have heard the story and did not allow it to keep them from their dream.

The young couple has researched Bigfoot online when they decided to buy the property and have continued looking up everything Bigfoot online trying to learn as much as they can.

Moving day comes and the young couple has family from both sides and friends helping them move in.

As they are moving in several people hear a Bigfoot roar including the young couple.

Everybody continues working on getting them moved in and it only takes one weekend with all the help. Now they just need to unpack and figure out where they will put everything. The entire weekend nobody saw a Bigfoot although many of the helpers wanted to see at least one.

The entire move was watched by the Bigfoots in the area even though the people never saw any of the Bigfoots.

The couple is on the back porch visiting with the neighbor that stopped by to greet them and offer any assistance they may need as they are starting out.

While visiting they hear a roar that rattles the windows of the house and they see a Bigfoot on the hill in the hay field.

Other Bigfoots respond to the roar and then the only one visible disappears as it walks away from the hill top and back to the woods.